The Mermaid Summer

The Mermaid Summer

by
MOLLIE HUNTER

Hamish Hamilton · London

HAMISH HAMILTON CHILDREN'S BOOKS
Published by the Penguin Group
27 Wrights Lane, London w8 5TZ, England
Viking Penguin Inc., 40 West 23rd Street, New York, New York 10010, USA
Penguin Books Australia Ltd, Ringwood, Victoria, Australia
Penguin Books Canada Ltd, 2801 John Street, Markham, Ontario, Canada
L3R 1B4
Penguin Books (NZ) Ltd, 182–190 Wairau Road, Auckland 10, New Zealand

Penguin Books Ltd, Registered Offices: Harmondsworth, Middlesex, England

First published 1988

Copyright © Maureen Mollie Hunter McIlwraith, 1988

British Library Cataloguing in Publication Data
Hunter, Mollie
Mermaid summer.
Rn: Maureen Mollie Hunter McIlwraith
I. Title
823'.914[J]   PZ7
ISBN 0-241-12225-2

Made and printed in Great Britain by
Richard Clay Ltd, Bungay, Suffolk
Filmset in Linotron Electra by
Rowland Phototypesetting Ltd,
Bury St Edmunds, Suffolk

To my great-niece, Catriona McVeigh
and my great-nephews Sean McVeigh and Leon McVeigh
With love from Mollie Hunter

Chapter One

About a hundred years ago, they say, there was a mermaid who ruled the cold, wild sea that washes around northern lands.

Nobody could tell how long she had been there before that time; but they did know that her favourite haunts were around some great pinnacles of rock that rose straight out of the seabed, and that were called "The Drongs". They knew also that she could cause strange and dangerous things to happen at sea; and so all the fishermen of those parts were always careful to speak well of her.

This was especially so, of course, in the fishing village that lay nearest to The Drongs – all except for one man who was not so wise in this as the rest of the men there. Eric Anderson, he was called, and he was a big man with a reddish-grey beard, and a gold earring in one ear. He also had a big laugh that people liked to hear; but nobody liked to hear the laugh he always gave whenever the mermaid happened to be mentioned.

"She might hear you," they warned, "and *then* you'll be in trouble!"

"I would," agreed Eric, "providing there *is* such a creature as a mermaid."

Now this was really a remarkable thing for any fisherman to say, because there are no people in the world, as a rule, who are as superstitious as fisher-folk. It was not the first time, however, that Eric Anderson had laughed at the odd beliefs of his fellow-fishermen – partly because he was a man of great common sense; but partly also, it has to be admitted, because he was just a bit too fond of a joke. As it happened too, there was not a single one of those other men who had ever doubted the mermaid's existence; and so, of course, they were all horrified at this kind of answer.

"But listen, man," they told him. "Any trouble that happens won't fall only on you. Just think of your wife, your son, your grandchildren. What will *they* do if the mermaid takes her revenge on you?"

Many times also, Eric's wife, Sarah, warned him in the same way, and so did their son, Robert, and Robert's wife, Kristine.

"Is it a widow you're wanting me to be?" Sarah asked him. "Because remember, that's what could happen if you're not more careful."

"Aye, and remember something else," chimed in Robert, "I have to share a boat with you – not to mention the three other men of our crew; and so what happens to you is just as likely to happen to the rest of us."

"Which means you're putting the happiness of other women and children at risk, the same as you're doing with ours," Kristine warned. And so the argument went on while the grandchildren, Jon and Anna, looked in fearful wonder from one to the other and tried to decide which of them had the right of it all. It was an argument, also, that always ended with Eric noticing the wondering eyes of the children, and once again laughing his great rich laugh as he told them:

"Ach, come on, now, there's no need for you two to be in a fright over all this! Because a mermaid, you see, is nothing more than a story for bairns like yourselves. But there's still no such thing as a woman with a fish's tail where her legs should be; and so, if anyone thinks *I* should be frightened of such a story, they just couldn't be more wrong."

It was Eric who was wrong in this, however, very wrong; and the proof of it came one winter's day when that grandson, Jon, was about ten, and the granddaughter, Anna, a year younger.

A fog came down over the sea that day, a fog that Eric and the crew of his boat knew would be dangerous for them if they did not get quickly into harbour. They had no compass to help them in this, either, because the small fishing boats of those days never did carry a compass.

With the coming of the fog, moreover, the wind had died – which meant that their sails were now useless. They still had two pairs of oars, however, and Eric could still see the crest of a hill and various other landmarks that he could use as guides to bring them homewards.

Quickly he set course by these landmarks, while his son, Robert, and the other three crewmen bent to the oars.

All four men pulled as hard as they could, and Eric kept his eyes fixed intently on the landmarks; but the fog rapidly grew so dense that, one by one, they disappeared from his view. Nearer at hand, also, the fog was swirling and rolling around the great pinnacles of The Drongs. Eric peered in that direction, hoping to take a fresh bearing from those pinnacles, and saw that there was some kind of creature perched on the lowest part of the rock. Puzzled, he looked more closely yet, and realised suddenly that it was not a seal – as he had thought at first it might be. It was the mermaid.

He rubbed his eyes, thinking the fog was playing tricks with his sight. Then he looked again – and still she was there! With horror as well as astonishment now making his eyes pop almost out of his head, he raised an arm to point at her.

"There!" he yelled. "Look there! It's the *mermaid!*"

Robert and the other three crewmen turned to look in the direction of his pointing hand. The fog was wreathing around the mermaid, making a ghostly sort of figure of her; but the figure was still undeniably that of a mermaid!

The crewmen stared at her in a horror that equalled Eric's own. Their oars came to rest. The boat began to drift. The movement of the tide carried the boat nearer to The Drongs, and nearer yet, before the danger of being wrecked there forced Eric to shake himself out of the trance that held him.

"Row!" he yelled, and swung the tiller to set course in a direction away from The Drongs. "Row now for your lives!"

Just as Eric had done, then, the other men shook themselves free of their trance of horror. They bent again to the oars, and began pulling away as hard as they could; but no sooner had they taken the first stroke of the new course Eric had set, than the mermaid began to sing.

"Don't listen!" Eric roared. "Stop your ears!" But how could they do that when they needed both hands to row? And how could Eric himself stop his ears when he needed to hold on to the tiller?

The fog covered the sight of the mermaid from them, but still she sang on, her voice as sweet as that of a nightingale in a midnight wood, as sad as that of a lost child crying, as thrilling as the voice of the last singer left alive anywhere, with the whole vast and empty world for its concert hall.

The heads of the oarsmen turned towards the sound of her singing. The sweetness of it fascinated them. Their hearts filled with pity at the sadness in it. The thrilling notes of her music filled their souls with yearning. It was a spell that drew them towards her, and even although each one of them knew this was so, there was nothing any of them could do to resist the power of that spell.

Their efforts at the oars grew slack. Then one by one, as the spell took complete hold on them, they shipped their oars; and with head bowed in bitter regret for all his past foolishness, Eric dropped his hold on the tiller as he, too, was finally overcome by the power of her spell.

The boat drifted again, with the waves once more carrying it closer and closer to the sharp pinnacles of The Drongs. And still the mermaid sang. But now, also, her voice had taken on a triumphant note that sent an even deeper chill through the listening men.

She was exulting in the terrible death she had planned for them, they realised; and with bitter hearts they realised also that she would never relent in that plan. Helplessly they waited for the final moment of their doom; and despairingly, as the boat was sucked into the fierce currents surging among The Drongs, they heard the mermaid end her song on a last piercingly high note of triumph.

The currents hurled their little wooden craft against the rock, splintering its sides, tossing Eric and his crew into the welter of white broken water – but also tossing out all the fishing gear the boat had held. And it was this, as it happened, that saved them then from drowning.

There were various things among that gear they could grab hold of – things that were like life-belts to them – such as the wickerwork creels that held their fishing lines, and the floats they used for buoying up the lines when these became heavy with fish.

Each one of them, then, made the desperate effort

that was needed to get hold of a creel or a float; but even after they had succeeded in that, they were still battered helplessly about by the whirlpool of water among The Drongs. For half an hour and more, this went on, with each man constantly being caught up in some huge swirl of water that dashed him against the rock, and each of them powerless to stop this happening.

The only thing that any of them could do, in fact, was to pray – which, you may be sure, was something that all of them did with all their might. And maybe it was this that saved them in the end, or maybe it was just the chance movements of these same fierce currents that threw them clear eventually of The Drongs – only to be faced then with yet another problem.

It was all very well being now in calmer water, with the chance of swimming for final safety; but the fog was still too thick to let them see the shore, and so how could they tell in which direction they should swim? And even supposing they could solve that problem, how could they force their bruised and battered bodies into the effort needed for swimming?

Well, as they say in these parts, "A man is kind to his life" – by which they mean that a man who faces certain death will take any action to avoid that fate, however little chance of success that action might offer.

And so, exhausted as they were by that time, Eric and all the other men continued to cling to their floats and creels; and despairing as they were of ever managing to reach land, they all tried to summon some small further strength for the movements needed to kick out in a direction they hoped would take them there.

Fortunately for them all, too, it was Eric who decided on that direction, and he did so by using the only possible method now open to them – the one that fogbound seamen of olden times had always been forced to rely on to find land. He watched out for the one big wave that happens in every seven, the one they called the "mother-wave"; because this wave is a directional one, and land always lies at right angles to it.

So they finally did reach the shore, all of them feeling more dead than alive, but still alive for all that. Yet even so, none of them was as grateful for Eric Anderson's help in this as they might otherwise have been. Because it was his jeering at the mermaid that had been the cause of it all in the first place – hadn't it? And there was still the reckoning to come for that!

Chapter Two

It was only two days afterwards that Eric had to face the reckoning; but first, because it was the custom in those parts when men had been saved from the sea, there was a service of thanksgiving in the village church.

Everyone in the village was there, from the youngest of children right up to The Oldest Fisherman – a white-bearded man called Jimsie Jamieson who was too old now to sail with the other fishermen.

Everyone sang lustily, especially when it came to "The Sailors' Hymn" – *Eternal Father, strong to save/ Whose arm doth bind the restless wave*; everyone, that is, except Eric Anderson, who was still feeling so guilty over the way he had nearly caused the death of all his crew that he had no heart at all for any kind of singing.

His silence was puzzling at first to his grandchildren, Jon and Anna; but then Anna understood the reason for it, and reached up a hand to rest in one of his hands. Anna always was quicker than Jon to understand such things, and that handclasp was her way of telling Eric that *she* didn't blame him for what had happened.

The poor, shamed man closed his big hand gratefully

around her small one. The congregation sang on. The music was slow and solemn. And what between this and the feeling she had for her grandfather, Anna felt the hair rising on the back of her neck when it came to the lines *O hear us when we cry to Thee/For those in peril on the sea.*

The mermaid, she thought, was the worst of all the perils of the sea now, for her Granda; and it was this thought of Anna's, in fact, that was the key to the reckoning he had to face at the meeting held by the fishermen once the church service was over. Robert Anderson was at that meeting too, of course, and when the two of them came home from it, there was nothing to choose between them for gloomy looks.

"There's not a man in the village will sail with me now," Eric told the others. "Not even my own son, here. Not that I blame even him for that, of course, because I know as well as all the other men do that there could only be bad luck for them now, with me in a boat beside them. What's more, that mermaid meant to drown me, for sure; and so, even if my mates *were* willing to have me with them, I could never again venture on the waters that they sail."

Sarah's thoughts flew immediately to Jimsie Jamieson, The Oldest Fisherman. "But that needn't matter so much," she comforted. "After all, Eric, there's some I could name that are perfectly happy to have retired from the sea."

"If you're thinking of old Jimsie," Eric told her

grimly, "I've better things yet to do with my life than sit on the harbour wall telling stories to bairns."

"What does that mean, then?" Sarah asked. "That you'll look for a shore job?"

"Not me," Eric told her. "The sea's in my blood, Sarah; and so, even if I did find a shore job, there would still surely come a day when I'd be tempted to sail these waters again."

"But if you don't retire, and if you don't get a shore job," Sarah insisted, "what *will* you do?"

"I'll sail on some ocean-going ship," said Eric. "I'll sign on for voyaging on foreign seas, far away from here; and so I'll be just as far away, too, from that mermaid. But you'll still be all right for money, Sarah, because I'll send you every penny I can spare from my wages, and—"

"Money!" Sarah screeched. "Am I to be thinking only about money and you leaving me to go maybe to the other end of the world?"

In great agitation then, Eric tugged at the gold earring in his left ear as he tried to think what to say next. "But Sarah," he protested at last, "what choice do I have? And what choice do you have if you don't want to risk the very thing you feared and wake up one day to find yourself a widow?"

Sarah cried aloud at this; and then, with her apron raised to her eyes, she rocked back and forward in her chair, weeping bitterly all the time she rocked. Robert and his wife Kristine glanced uncomfortably at one another; and after a moment, Kristine also burst into tears. Jon and Anna looked solemnly on, neither of them knowing what to make of all this; and as for Eric himself, his distress was as great as Sarah's. But he, poor soul, had the old-fashioned idea that men are not supposed to weep; and so he had to choke back the tears that he, too, would otherwise have shed.

Nothing else that was said after that, however, could persuade him to change his decision. But one thing he did agree to do before he carried out that decision was to go and see the woman they called "the Howdy", who was the local wise woman, and who sometimes also knew things that other people could not be expected to know – things that might happen in the future.

"So?" asked Sarah when he came back from this visit. "What did the Howdy tell you?"

"She told me," said Eric, "that it's right for me to go. That the mermaid will always be a danger to me if I stay. But beyond that she could not see – or maybe it was me that was at fault, because all her talk beyond that was in riddles I could not understand. And so there's still nothing for it, Sarah. I *have* to go; and the sooner I do that, the better it will be for us all."

"You're stubborn, Eric," cried Sarah. "Oh, but you're a stubborn man!"

Eric went to pack his kitbag without making any answer to this. Jon and Anna ran to help him gather the things he needed to put in it, and it was while she was helping like this that Anna took the chance to ask wistfully:

"Granda Eric, does this mean we'll never see you again?"

"Well, now," said Eric, and managed to raise a smile for her benefit, "'never' is a big word, eh? And so why do we not just say that I'll come back home again just as soon as somebody has managed to tame that mermaid. And who knows? That could just happen yet. Couldn't it, now?"

It could, Anna supposed, but it didn't seem likely to her, or to Jon either – and even less so to the others there. It was altogether a sad little party, then, that saw Eric on his way the next day, kitbag on his shoulder, his one gold earring glinting in the morning sunlight. And long after their farewells had been said, they stood watching him stride out along the road that led south to the big port where he hoped to sign on for his first voyage on an ocean-going ship.

Further and further away he strode, turning every now and then to give them yet another wave of good-bye; and each time he did so they could see the sun catching yet another glint of gold from his earring. Then he was too far away for them to see that glint. Soon afterwards, a bend of the road took him completely out of their sight, and there was nothing left for them to do but to get on as best as they could without him.

And without a boat, too, as Robert reminded them; because a fisher family without a boat is like a bird with broken wings. The bird cannot fly. The fisher cannot put to sea. And so, when it comes to finding a living, one is as helpless as the other. On the other hand, it has to be said, there are no people more ready to help one another than fisher folk; and it was on the very next day after Eric had gone that Robert Anderson had the offer of a boat from Jimsie Jamieson, The Oldest Fisherman.

"Because," said Jimsie, "I'm not only Eric Anderson's good friend. I'm also The Oldest Fisherman – which gives me a duty, Robert, to you younger men. Besides which, I've no use for my boat now I've retired from the sea. And so away you go and gather Eric's old crew, along with one other man to replace him. Then you shall have that boat of mine for as long as it takes to earn enough from it to buy another one of your own."

"And you shall have an equal share of each catch we make from it!" Gratefully, Robert assured Jimsie of this – because this was always the way it was with these fishermen and their boats. Each day's catch was always divided into equal shares, with one share going to each man in the boat and one share to its owner.

Jimsie's offer, all the same, had still been made in kindness; but being a poor man, he was naturally pleased to find Robert sticking to the usual arrangement. And so they parted, with both men happy about its terms. Robert went off to round up his crew; and very soon after that, life was going on for him and his family much as it had been before Eric's departure.

Each day at low tide, Kristine dug the sand to find lug-worms for bait. Sarah helped her to bait the miles of fishing line Robert would use, with Jon and Anna to lend a hand in this as soon as school was over for the day. In the small hours of each morning Robert rose from his warm bed to gather his crew for the long, cold hours they would spend out at the fishing-grounds. Then, when the boat came home, Kristine and Sarah cleaned their family's share of the catch.

Some of this they kept for their own use. Some of it they prepared for selling later on in the nearest town, either by packing it in salt or by hanging it up in their smokehouse to be turned into smoked fish. Twice a week, also, they filled their big carrying creels with the fresh fish and tramped miles to sell this to the farm folk who lived inland from the village.

It was hard work every day for them all, in fact; but they were used to hard work, and so that did not bother them. The rest of that winter fishing season went by, also, without any of them once seeing or hearing anything of the mermaid – which should have meant, of course, that they now had nothing at all to worry them. But that was not so, because now they had one new worry.

The worry was Sarah!

She was not well – she had not been well, in fact, since Eric had gone away; and though it was only small ailments that bothered her, they could all see how miserable she was.

So there came a day when Kristine decided to fetch the Howdy to see her – because the Howdy was not only the wise woman of the village. She also had what they called *eolas*, a magical skill in healing; and for everything that had gone wrong with Sarah, the Howdy had some herb or other to help her in her charms – foxglove for skin rashes, eyebright for sore eyes, yarrow for the staunching of blood, and so on.

Jon and Anna, however, had always been terribly afraid of the Howdy with her sharp eyes and sly, knowing smile; and so, as soon as they saw her near the door of their house, they were both off like a shot. The Howdy watched them go, not showing any expression on her face – she being well used to seeing children dart out of her path. Then into the house she went, took a good look at Sarah's pale face and dejected air, and immediately told Kristine:

"Fetch me water."

Kristine brought a cup of water. The Howdy took from her pocket the stone she called her "healing stone" – which was a small piece of white quartz, very smooth and shiny. She dropped this healing stone into the water. She muttered some words over the cup, then held it out to Sarah and said:

"Sip this."

Cautiously, Sarah took some sips from the cup. The Howdy sprinkled the remaining water over her, put her healing stone away again, and then told Sarah:

"Now you have been cured of all your ills. But

something else I must tell you, is this. The cure will not last if you go on despairing of seeing Eric again, because it is from despair that all your ailments have come."

"What are you saying, Howdy?" Sarah exclaimed. "That there is hope I *will* see him again?"

"There is always hope for everything," the Howdy told her. "And hope is always the best medicine."

"But the mermaid!" Sarah exclaimed. "What about the mermaid?"

"All I can tell you of that," said the Howdy, "is that everything which is still to happen about Eric and the mermaid will concern the number three. But more than that I cannot say, because even to me, you understand, the things that are still to happen can be revealed only a little at a time."

Off she went then, leaving Sarah with the beginnings of hope that Eric's departure might not finally be the disaster it had seemed to her. Yet still, she wondered, what on earth could the number three possibly have to do with him and the mermaid?

For long, that day, she and Kristine puzzled over this. For long that day also, the Howdy sat in her own house trying to peer even further into the future. But the Howdy liked the feeling of power it gave her to know things that other people did not know; and so, when she did at last get another glimpse of the future, she told no one what or who she had seen there.

Even so, however, she could not help smiling the next time she saw Jon and Anna running out of her path.

And the smile she gave then was a sly and knowing one –
the very smile, in fact, that had always made them both
so afraid of her.

Chapter Three

Now whether or not it was the Howdy's healing stone that cured Sarah of her ailments, it was certainly true that her health never once looked back after that visit.

Eric was as good as his word, too, in sending money to her; and so she was further cheered by the letters that eventually began to arrive along with the money. Then, at the end of the summer when Jon was eleven and Anna was ten – which was about nine months after Eric's departure – he did better than write. He sent a present to each member of the family.

The presents came in a box that had a large number of brightly-coloured foreign postal stamps on it, and the first present they opened was for Robert. It was a compass – "So that you'll never again have to depend on the mother-wave to guide you in a fog," wrote Eric in the letter that came with the presents.

Kristine's present was a brooch made of silver inset with a single large and gleaming white pearl. Anna's present was a necklace of pale pink coral. For Jon, there was a shell, a great big shell shaped like that of a whelk.

The outside of it was rough and pinkish-brown in colour. Inside, it was a smooth and glowing pink.

"They call this kind of shell a 'conch'," said Eric's letter. "And if you blow into one end of it like the natives hereabouts do, it will give out a sound like the sound of a trumpet."

The very last present to be opened was for Sarah, and it was a lace shawl of purest white, very cunningly woven with a pattern of flowers; and of this shawl Eric wrote:

"I'd never before seen a shawl that could pass the test of the ones you knit – not until I saw this one! Try it and see."

Sarah laughed at this and pulled off her wedding ring because – like all fisherwives, of course, she could knit lacey-patterned shawls in very fine wool; and her test of success in this was to finish up with a shawl so delicate in texture that she could draw the whole of it through her wedding ring.

Everyone gathered round to see her put the white lace shawl to this test, but the threads of it were so cobweb-fine that there wasn't the slightest doubt of her being able to draw it easily through the ring; and it was while the rest of the family were laughing at this and admiring once more the beauty of the shawl, that Jon slipped out of doors with *his* present.

"The sound of a trumpet" – that's what his Granda Eric had said he could get from the conch shell. And he was desperate to find out if that was true!

Down to the harbour he ran, carefully hiding the

conch from view by thrusting it up inside his gansey –
the dark-blue woollen sweater that was the common
dress of boys and men alike in fisher villages. By keeping
it secret like that, he reckoned, he could give his
schoolmates all the more of a surprise when it finally
came to showing-off the sound he hoped to get from the
conch; and it was with this in mind, too, that he went on
past the harbour till he reached the rocky foreshore on its
northward side.

Right out to the edge of the rocks he went, right to the
point where deep water lapped against them. Carefully
then, he looked around to make sure he was quite alone.
There was no-one else on the rocks; no-one between
himself and the village. He looked seaward, out over
water that was as blue as the blue summer sky above it.

Nothing moved on the sea either, nothing except gold
sparkles of sun on the broken water around The Drongs.
Jon took the conch shell out from underneath his
gansey, raised it to his lips, and blew into one end of it.

Nothing came out of the shell except a sound that was
between puffing and wheezing. Jon tried again, chang-
ing the position of his lips around the end of the shell;
and this time he got a sort of moaning sound from it. He
was beginning to get the hang of the proper way to blow,
he thought, and tried again, but still got only the
moaning sound. A fourth time he tried, then a fifth, and
this last time the conch gave out a sound that startled
him.

It was deep, and it was mournful – a sound like that of

a captive bull sadly bellowing; but it was also a loud and weirdly powerful sound, and Jon was delighted with it. Once again he sent out the same call, and then again, before he lowered the conch and stood trying to get his breath back.

"I'll show them!" he told himself, thinking exultantly of the envy of his schoolmates when they heard him blowing the conch. "I'll show them!"

He raised the conch to his lips for one last blow before he went racing homewards with it; and just as he did so there was a flash of silver in the broken water among The Drongs. The flash was followed by a tremendous burst of spray rising from the sea between The Drongs and the place where he stood on the rocks; and greatly puzzled by all this, Jon lowered the conch to stand staring at the place where the spray had arisen.

It had to be a mighty big fish, thought he, to make a splash like that! But what kind of a fish? A basking shark, maybe? It was true that basking sharks were sometimes seen off that coast, and they certainly were big fish; big enough, in fact, to overturn a fishing boat if one of them decided to charge it – which, indeed, Jon knew, was something that had happened more than once to various of the boats from the village. And he had never seen a basking shark before, so now was maybe his chance!

For long minutes after this thought had occurred to him, Jon stood waiting in the hope that the basking shark, or whatever it was, would swim close enough to the rocks for him to get a sight of it. Nothing happened.

The gold-tipped swirl of water around The Drongs danced as before. The rest of the sea remained calm, with a shine on its unbroken surface like the shine of blue glass.

Jon began to wonder if he should take time for another blow at his conch shell, or whether he should race home there and then to boast about it to Anna. His gaze, travelling inwards from scanning the sea, came to rest on the water that lapped the rock on which he stood. The lapping water swirled into sudden movement. "The fish!" Jon thought. "I'm going to see the fish, after all!" But the creature that surfaced from that swirl of water, was the mermaid.

Her head came first, then her hands came up to grip the edge of the rock. The hands had nails of the same pale pink as Anna's coral necklace. The hair streaming down on either side of her face was the dark-gold colour of wet sand. This was all that Jon was able to realise in the shock of that first moment of seeing her. And so close to him, too! Hurriedly he backed a step, then would have turned and run except that he was too fascinated by her to do so.

Her face, he noticed then, was the colour of the pearl in his mother's new brooch – white, yet with a lustrous glow to its pallor. Her eyes were green; but how could you describe such a green – so deep, so dark, so full of some terrible inner fire! And those same eyes, so beautiful yet so frightening were staring at him, staring in a way that made his inside quiver with fear. Yet still, it

29

seemed, he could not call up the will to turn and run from her.

He thought of his grandfather's boat being wrecked on The Drongs, and his fear grew even greater. Questions leapt into his mind. Would she sing to him? And would her song be the same deathly one she had sung to Granda Eric? The mermaid opened her coral-pink lips; but to his great wonder then, instead of singing she spoke to him, and to his even greater wonder what she said was:

"Well, what d'you want? Why did you summon me?"

Summon her? Jon gaped, his thoughts in a whirl, and finally managed to stammer, "I – I – didn't. I mean, how could *I* summon *you*?"

The strange green of the mermaid's eyes sparked angrily. "But you did. You know you did."

"I don't know anything of the kind," Jon protested fearfully. "All I did was blow this thing here – the conch shell."

"Three times," the mermaid reminded him. "Three times you blew the conch. And so you *did* summon me, because the three-times sound of a conch shell is the call that all mermaids must answer."

"I didn't know that," Jon confessed. "I – I'm sorry. I just didn't know."

The mermaid stared at him, the fire in her eyes beginning to die down until it was replaced by a look of contempt. "Land-creatures!" she said scathingly. "They're all like you – stupid. They don't know anything."

"I won't do it again." Jon could still feel his insides quivering with fear of this strange sea-creature, and so he said this very humbly; but the mermaid, it seemed, was not entirely satisfied with this assurance.

"If you do," she warned, "and if it turns out that your call was without cause, you had better stick to the land, because never again will you be safe at sea."

On the word "sea", her hands released their grip on the rock. She slid downwards, her hair swirling for a moment on the water's surface before her head disappeared from Jon's view.

The next moment, however, he saw the whole length of her tail flicking upwards out of the water in a sparkle of scales that flashed in the sun like a firework display of blue and green and silver. The glittering tail gave a last flash as it speared cleanly downwards in the dive that took her finally back into the depths of the sea. And it was only then, with the knowledge that she was really gone, that Jon found he was able to turn and run.

Panting, scrambling, leaping from rock to rock, and finally racing madly over the stretch of shingle between rock and harbour, he made his way homewards; but he was still only halfway there when a sudden thought slowed him to a halt. Supposing he told the rest of the family what had happened – as he had certainly meant to do, up till that moment. What would they say?

It was true he hadn't intended to summon the mermaid. But maybe they wouldn't take that as an excuse. Maybe they would still blame him for causing her to appear again. Maybe they would fear that it would bring bad luck to the new boat his father had finally managed to buy to replace the old one Jimsie Jamieson had loaned him. And maybe that was exactly what *would* happen!

Jon felt his inward quivering begin again as he stood and considered all these questions; and when he remembered the angry green of the mermaid's eyes, he quivered even more. But a decision still had to be made before he reached home again; and, as it happened, the decision he finally came to was that he would say nothing at all about having summoned the mermaid. And that way, he reckoned, he would not be blamed for anything that might happen as a result of having done so.

It was not a brave decision to take, of course – quite the opposite in fact; but Jon, it has to be remembered, was only just eleven years old at this time, and it can be very difficult at that age to take brave decisions. Also as it happened, he did not reach home that day until he had met unexpectedly with the Howdy; so unexpectedly, in fact, that he had no chance to run from her as he would otherwise have done.

There was no chance either of hiding the conch shell from her, because her eyes went immediately to the bulge it made under his gansey, and nothing would satisfy her but to be given a sight of it. Very unwillingly, then, Jon showed her the shell.

"It's a present from my granda," he explained. "He sent presents to all of us."

"Indeed," the Howdy exclaimed. "Did he so! And what, pray, were those other presents?"

"A shawl," Jon told her, "a compass, a silver brooch, and a coral necklace."

"Oh, aye?" the Howdy said thoughtfully. "The shawl for your granny, eh? The compass for your father, the brooch for your mother, and the necklace for your wee sister – is that right?" Jon nodded, wondering what was coming next, and was not long left in doubt.

"Well now," the Howdy told him. "Heed me, boy. Of all these presents it is only the shell that is important to you and yours. And so take care of it. Take very good care!"

On she went, then, with her fat little figure in its black dress looking, all of a sudden, mysteriously dark against the brightness of the day. Jon stared after her, wondering what on earth she had meant about the shell being the only thing that was important to him and his family; and the more he wondered about this, the more nervous it made him.

When he got home, he vowed to himself, he would not only hide from his family the fact that he had summoned the mermaid. He would put the conch shell itself away in some hiding-place, and never take it out again. Or not until he had some reason for doing so, anyway – and considering what had happened with his granda and the mermaid, that reason would certainly have to be a very good one!

Chapter Four

"I'm going to write to Granda Eric," said Anna, "to thank him for my present."

"Oh, aye?" her mother asked, "and where, pray, will you send your letter?"

Where, indeed? It was a question that simply had not occurred to Anna before then, and so she was quite taken aback by it.

It was true, of course, that there had been a number of letters from her grandfather by that time. But all of these had been very short ones that just told briefly where he had been. There was never anything in them of where he might be going; not even the name of his ship, not so much as a hint of any address for letters they might want to send to him!

"And," said Sarah, "I know the reason for that, because your grandfather had a private word with me about it before he left. He just doesn't want to get letters from us in case they make him feel so homesick that he wouldn't be able to resist coming back here."

Now Sarah could not have said anything more likely to make Anna even more determined to write to her grandfather because, the truth of the matter was, there was a great attachment between her and Eric. They had a lot in common, after all, both of them being very warm-hearted – not to mention strong-willed; and so it was only natural that Anna should have continued to miss him just as much as she had when he had first left home.

Once Anna had been struck by an idea, also, there was no way she could be stopped from carrying out that idea. So she thought, and better thought, of how she would send the letter she meant to write; and when she had finally come to a decision on this, she got hold of Jon and told him:

"I *am* going to write to Granda Eric. And what I'll do with the letter is to put it into a bottle. Then I'll throw the bottle into the sea, and it'll sail and sail till it's washed up on some faraway coast. And whoever finds it then and sees the letter in it might just be the very one who knows where Granda Eric is; and so they'll give it to him."

Well, this was such a far-fetched idea, of course, that Jon simply laughed at it. But still Anna persisted in arguing with him that it could just work, it might just work; and, in the end, he grew so impatient with this that he told her: "Now listen here, Anna. We'll go and see Jimsie Jamieson, because he's The Oldest Fisherman and there's nobody knows more about the sea than he does. And if *he* says your idea is nonsense, you'll just have to believe him. Will you not?"

"I will," agreed Anna. And so off the two of them

went to see The Oldest Fisherman, and found him as usual, sitting on the harbour wall with his long, lean figure bent over the piece of soapstone he was carving with some figure of the sea. As usual, too, he was ready to tell a story to anyone who would listen – because Jimsie Jamieson had not always been a fisherman. In his young days, he had sailed the seven seas of the world, and he was full of tales about the adventures of all that voyaging.

Strange tales they were, too, quite good enough to go into a book, some of them – like, for instance, the one about the time he had hunted the Great White Shark off the coast of Australia. Or even better, perhaps, the one that told of how he had been alone on deck one night when the Great Sea Serpent itself had reared its monstrous head from the water—

"But it's not a story we're wanting just now," Anna explained when Jimsie offered them the choice of these two tales. "It's an argument we want you to settle, Jimsie."

"Let's hear your problem, then," invited Jimsie – who was as good at listening as he was at talking; and laying aside his carving, he sat in silence while Anna told of her idea for sending a letter to Eric and of the way Jon had disagreed with her over this. To her great disappointment at the end of it all, however, Jimsie shook his head and said gently:

"I'm sorry, lass, but Jon has told you truly. Throw a bottle into the sea here, and there's no way it could fetch up on the coast of any of those faraway lands where your Granda might be."

"But why not?" Anna argued. "Why wouldn't it just sail and sail till it reached one of those lands?"

"Because," said Jimsie patiently, "the tide that rises and falls in our northern sea would have brought it back to this coast long before it could sail far enough to reach one of the great ocean currents that could carry it to any distant part of the world. That's why. But there's still no need to despair, lass – if you just let me consider for a bit, that is."

For a few moments after that, Jimsie sat stroking thoughtfully at his bushy white beard. Then he picked up his carving again, and Anna became impatient to hear what he would say next. Jimsie, she knew, told all his best stories when he was carving soapstone with the figures of whales and mermaids and other creatures of the sea. But that was also when he always had his best ideas.

Jimsie turned his block of soapstone over in his huge old hands, studied the figure of the dolphin he had been carving on it, and then began putting some extra touches to it.

"Tell me something about those letters from your Granda," said he. "Did the stamps on the envelopes show that they had all been sent from foreign lands?"

Jon and Anna looked at one another, both of them thinking back to seeing the envelopes that had held Eric's letters; and after a minute Jon said, "I remember one with a stamp that showed it was posted in this country – one that came about three months ago."

"And the very first one he ever wrote," said Anna, "the one he sent just a week after he left here – that had the same kind of stamp on it too."

"Well, now," Jimsie told them, "that first letter would very likely be posted from the port where he first set sail. And so tell me, now, if you can remember the postmark that was on the envelope."

Anna closed her eyes and thought of the envelope with its stamp and the round postmark that showed the name of the place where Eric's first letter had been posted.

A picture grew behind her closed eyes, a picture that showed two envelopes – the one that had held the first letter, and the one that had held the letter of three months ago. She saw Eric's handwriting on both the envelopes. She saw the stamps on them. She saw the name of the postmark on each of them; and in each case it was the name of a big seaport that lay far to the south of her own village. She saw everything clearly, and with her eyes flying wide open again, she exclaimed:

"*I* remember! I remember the postmark on both the letters. And it was the same on each of them." Promptly then, she gave Jimsie the name of the big port, and the instant she spoke it, a gleam of satisfaction came into his faded old eyes. He smiled, looking first at her, and then at Jon.

"Listen, then," said he, "while I explain something to you. The postmark on that letter you got three months ago tells us that your Granda must have come back to the port where he posted the first one he sent you – back to the port he first sailed from. D'you understand?"

Jon and Anna nodded to show him they did understand, and Jimsie went on, "Well then, to a sailor, that can mean only one thing. That port must be the *home* port for the ship he has chosen; the one his ship comes back to at the end of every voyage. And so, Anna, the chances are that he'll come back to it again and again. And *that* is where you can send any letters you write to him."

"But Jimsie," Anna protested, "I can't send a letter with only my Granda's name and the name of a seaport on the envelope. He'd never get it if I did that."

"Of course he wouldn't," Jimsie agreed. "But when he comes ashore there between voyages, he'll do as every other deepsea sailor does till his ship's ready to put to sea again. He'll stay at the Seamen's Mission. And so all you have to do is to mark your letter 'To be collected' —"

"And to address it to him there!" burst in Anna, so excited as the meaning of Jimsie's words broke on her that she could not wait for him to finish speaking. She was away on the instant then, calling her thanks over her shoulder as she went. Jimsie watched her go, smiling at her eagerness, and then turned to ask Jon:

"And what about you, eh? Will you write to your Granda too, now, to thank him for your present?"

39

"I'll think about it," said Jon, uneasily remembering the conch shell still lying in the hiding-place he had found for it.

What could he say about the shell, he wondered, supposing he did write to his grandfather? Because he couldn't write *without* mentioning it, could he? And yet, how could he mention the conch without the risk of giving away his secret about the mermaid? He couldn't chance that, Jon decided; and added lamely to his answer, "But I'm not very good at writing letters."

"Well, you could always add your name to the end of Anna's letter, couldn't you?" suggested Jimsie; and with some relief then, Jon decided that this was what he *would* do.

Anna was already busy writing by the time he had followed her home, and he was all ready with his answer when she looked up to ask him if he wanted to add anything to her letter.

"Oh, just my name," said he airily, and sat waiting until she was ready to pass the finished letter over to him. He signed his name then, under the place where she had ended it, *Please come home soon. Love. Anna.* Anna put the letter in an envelope, sealed this, and wrote the address on it; after which she showed it to the rest of the family – thinking, of course, that they would also be pleased to know this address.

"Because it'll let you write your own letters to Granda now," said she, once she had explained about discovering the address from Jimsie. But none of the others, it seemed, had any intentions at all of writing their own letters.

"And so far as I'm concerned, at least," Sarah informed her firmly, "that decision is a final one. If your Granda has chosen to arrange matters so that he thinks we won't be able to write to him, then I certainly don't intend to go roundabout to try and defeat that arrangement."

"Nor do I," chimed in Robert. "You won't get me trying to meddle with fate!"

"Besides which," Kristine added, "it could all be just a waste of time anyway – because how could anyone believe the kind of nonsense talked by old Jimsie Jamieson?"

"Indeed, Kristine," Sarah exclaimed, "you're right about that! And I'm surprised at you, Anna, paying any attention to him when you know he'll say anything to you just so long as he thinks it'll make a good story!"

It was odd, Anna thought then, that neither her mother nor her grandmother seemed able to tell the difference between Jimsie when he was story-telling just for the fun of it, and Jimsie when he was using his great knowledge of the sea to say something quite serious.

As for her letter being a waste of time, she was so far from believing this to be the case that, for weeks after she had sent it off, she could think of nothing else except how soon her grandfather might get it. She spoke so often to Jimsie about this, in fact, that he was forced finally to warn her it could be months rather than weeks before this happened.

"Maybe even longer than that," he added, "because your Granda might be away on a really long voyage when it arrives at the Seamen's Mission. And so it could even be years before he has a chance to get your letter."

"But he will get it in the end," Anna insisted. "He must, Jimsie, because I want so much that he should get it. And not just this one either, because I'm going to keep on writing to him."

"I believe you will," Jimsie said thoughtfully. "I do believe you will." And indeed he was right in this because, once she had set her mind to a thing, Anna Anderson was every bit as stubborn as her Granda Eric.

Faithfully after that, she went on writing to him, always finishing up the way she had finished the first letter, and then persuading Jon to add his name under the place where she had written, *Please come home soon. Love. Anna.* Always too, she kept hoping she would get an answer to one of her letters – especially when the postmark on one of his letters showed that he had been back to his home port. And even although she never did get an answer, she still persisted in writing to him.

It was not only when other presents arrived from him, either, that she wrote these further letters. Indeed, there were big gaps of time between the arrival of one present and the next. And so, the rest of the family gradually came to realise, it was something quite other than these that kept Anna so determinedly continuing with her letters.

If they had asked her, of course, she would have told them the truth, which was simply that she still hoped against hope that her letters would indeed persuade him to come home again. Also, writing letters just happened to be something she enjoyed – probably because she was rather good at it. But even so, there still came a time when she was puzzled to know what to say in one of her letters to Eric – the one she wrote after the first of those other presents arrived.

Chapter Five

There were a number of odd things about this other present. First of all, the paper the present was wrapped in carried no name to say who it was for. Also, in the letter they found inside the parcel, Eric gave no hint of the answer to this mystery. Then there was the present itself, which was a piece of very fine silk that might have been meant as a dress length.

"Although Eric can't have meant it to be made into a dress for me," Sarah declared, "because even he would know, surely, that I'm far too old to wear such a colour."

"And it can't be for me either," decided Kristine, "any more than it's for you. We're fishermen's wives, after all, and a dress made of this stuff is just not for the likes of us. Silk like this is for a gown for some grand lady to wear on some grand occasion – except that there isn't enough of it to make a gown for a full-grown woman."

"So who on earth can it be for?" Sarah wondered again; and decided finally to invite the Howdy to the house so that she could pose this same question to her.

"Just look at it," she invited, bringing out the silk for

the Howdy's inspection. "Is that not fit for a queen to wear?"

"It is," the Howdy agreed, her little eyes fairly snapping with curiosity. "And believe me, Sarah, it's a queen who *will* wear it!"

Sarah and Kristine exchanged glances of wonder at this, before Sarah asked, "And pray, Howdy, what do you mean by that?"

The Howdy, however, had no intention of explaining her remark. "You'll know in good time," was all she would say; and so there was nothing for it except to put the silk away again and try to forget the whole matter.

Anna and Jon, meanwhile, had been as careful as ever in keeping out of the house so long as the Howdy was there. Once she had gone, however, they came back in to find Sarah and Kristine still puzzling over her remark about the silk. And so, what between that and the general mystery it posed, there was little wonder that Anna herself was puzzled to know how to mention it in her next letter to Eric – except to say, of course, that the colour of it was strange, yet still very beautiful.

Jon would have been able to tell her a thing or two about this colour, however, if she had thought to ask him; because the moment that Jon saw the silk he had been reminded of all the colours that had flashed from the mermaid's tail as she dived back into the water.

The silk, in fact, was not just one colour. It was a blend of blues and greens and silver, with the blues and greens shading from the darkest of these colours to the lightest, and the silver rippling among them like the silver ripple of their own northern sea in the bright, icy days of winter.

But Anna, of course, had no reason to say anything to Jon about the silk; and for his part, Jon felt he had good reason for keeping quiet over anything to do with its colour. He could not mention this, after all, without confessing about the way he had summoned the mermaid with his conch shell. And when he remembered the anger in her eyes then, he was afraid once more that she might still be offended enough to cause harm to his father's boat.

Once more also, therefore, he felt guilty over what he had done. And so he hid his thoughts about the silk as carefully as he had hidden the conch itself, not telling these thoughts even to Anna – who was certainly some-one he *could* have trusted with a secret.

As time went by, too, and his father's boat continued safe from the disaster he had feared might happen to it, he found it becoming easier and easier for him to forget altogether about his meeting with the mermaid. In addition to which, the passing of time also gave him something else to think about in the shape of the next lot of presents from his grandfather.

For Anna, this time, there was a round hand-mirror, framed in silver, and with a handle also made of silver. The frame was carved into the shape of a circle of flower petals. The handle had been made to look like the stem of a flower, with leaves carved on it, and leaf-shapes springing from the top of it. The reflection of a face in this mirror, therefore, was like that of a face seen at the heart of a silver flower supported by a silver stem. But handsome as Anna's present was, Jon thought, it was still nothing compared to *his* present!

This was a knife in a leather sheath with a pattern of ships of all kinds stamped on the leather. And such a knife! The blade of it was long and curved, and so sharp that Robert Anderson was afraid at first to let his son handle it, never mind fasten the leather sheath on to his belt and swagger around the village with it the way he wanted to do.

"I don't know," he said doubtfully. "It's no toy, that knife. It's a tool, and a dangerous one at that for someone who doesn't know how to use it."

"But I can learn to use it, can't I?" Jon protested. "I'm good with my hands – you know I am. And besides, what about that apprenticeship in the boatyard that's been promised to me as soon as I'm old enough to leave school? I'll be handling sharp tools every day then, won't I? And so the sooner I do learn to do that the better it will be for me."

Now this was an argument that Robert Anderson could hardly deny, especially since it was perfectly true that Jon was naturally very skilful at working with his hands. Also, he was already big and strong for his age; and because he loved to work with the kind of wood used in the boatyard, he was very keen indeed to start his apprenticeship. It did seem only sensible then, Robert decided eventually, to allow him to get accustomed to using this fearsomely sharp knife – but only once he had been properly warned about it.

"Well," he agreed, "you could be right in what you say, and so I suppose I could let you start using it. But you've got my permission, remember, only if you keep carefully in mind that you must treat it as a tool, and not as a plaything."

"I will," Jon promised; and was so delighted with even this grudging permission, that he did more than just sign his name at the end of the letter Anna wrote to thank Eric for sending her the silver mirror.

Instead, he added a long postscript to this letter, telling Eric that he was especially pleased to have the knife because he was not going to be a fisherman when he left school. He was going to learn to build ships like the ships in the pattern on the sheath, and the knife would give him practice in the careful handling of the sharp tools he would have to use.

"But meanwhile," he finished proudly, "all the other boys here are very envious of me because there isn't one of them has a knife anything like mine!"

So this letter went to join all the others Anna had sent; and more time yet went by without her getting an answer to any of them. Then, in the year that John became thirteen and she became twelve, one further present arrived for her; and what Eric had sent her this time was a comb – but such a comb!

It was big, and curved, the kind that ladies of olden

times used to wear as an ornament in their hair. Its colour was green, a dark and glowing green; and Anna was quite enchanted to think how well this would look against the dark red of her hair.

"I want to try it," she said eagerly. "I want to see how it looks on me," and rushed straight away to get her silver mirror. Kristine helped her to unbraid her long hair and pile it all up on the top of her head. Then Anna herself fixed the comb into the pile of hair, and was quite awed to see the way it sat there, like a green crown shining on her head.

The comb, however, had quite a different effect on Jon; because once again he saw in it something that reminded him of the mermaid. That dark and glowing green, he recognised, was exactly the green of the mermaid's eyes. The memory of the angry fire he had seen in those eyes rushed over him; and feeling afraid the others might guess something from the expression on his face, he went hastily out of the house, leaving Kristine and Anna still admiring the comb and still talking about it.

"The stuff this comb is made of," Kristine was telling Anna, "is called 'jade', which makes it very precious; and that's a good reason for you to keep it very carefully. But an even better reason, maybe, is that your Granda must have looked very hard for a good present to send before he found something as unusual as this for you."

Kristine need not have bothered with all these warnings, however, because Anna had fallen so completely in love with the green jade comb that she was already vowing she would keep it to the end of her days, and always, always cherish it as the best of all possible presents she could have had from her Granda Eric.

On the following Sunday, also, when they were all getting ready for church, she persuaded her mother to let her wear it – not perched grandly on top of her head, of course, but just tucked modestly into the braids of hair hanging down her back. And that was how the Howdy came to notice it, as she too sat in church, with her sharp eyes as usual on the watch for anything that might be useful for her to know.

She noted the knife at Jon's belt also, just as she had already noted it when he first began wearing it around the village; and all through the service, after that, her eyes kept coming back to the comb and the knife. Then, when the service was over, she hurried out of church and stood waiting for Sarah and Kristine to appear.

"Aye, then," she greeted them, stepping right into their path. "I've a question for you, Sarah – about the girl's comb and the boy's knife. Were they presents from Eric?"

"They were," said Sarah; and eagerly then the Howdy asked, "And what else has he sent apart from these – and the ones I already know about, of course."

"A mirror," Sarah told her. "A silver mirror, for Anna."

"Ah-h-h!" The Howdy drew a deep breath of satisfaction. "I told you, didn't I," said she, "that everything to do with Eric and the mermaid would concern the number 3?" – Sarah nodded her agreement to this, and the Howdy went on,

"Well now, listen to this. This is the third year that Eric has been gone, and the presents he has sent since he left are now nine in number – the white shawl, the compass, the silver brooch, the coral necklace, the conch shell, the strange silk, the silver mirror, the knife, and the green comb!"

"What of that?" Sarah demanded; and swiftly the Howdy retorted:

"Nine, Sarah, is three times three. Also, it is one third of that nine – three things – that will matter in the end; and these three are the conch shell, the knife and the comb. What is more, the number three will once again rule Eric's fate, because it is in three months time that everything concerning him will be resolved one way or another."

Sarah stared in bewilderment at the Howdy. Her bewilderment gave way to anger at the woman's mysterious way of speaking; and Kristine also felt the same anger rising in her mind. In spite of the trust she had in the Howdy's healing powers, in fact, Kristine had always disliked this strange little woman; and so now she was pleased when Sarah said sharply:

"You'll have to speak plainer than that, Howdy. Because, I'm telling you now, you've spoken too much in riddles already. And I'm getting tired of such talk."

"I can only speak what I know," the Howdy defended

herself. "And even to me, Sarah, the future is not always fully known."

Kristine's dislike of the Howdy boiled over suddenly; and as sharply as Sarah had spoken, she said, "Yet you speak as if there was danger in it."

"Oh, there's danger, all right," the Howdy agreed. "I cannot tell you what that danger is – but I can smell it, just like those with my powers always can smell danger."

Kristine thought of her husband, her children, and her heart seemed to turn to stone in her breast. Hoarsely she asked, "And this danger – who does it threaten? Is it my man? Or my bairns?"

"It threatens you all," the Howdy said, "every man, woman and child in this village. But do not ask me any more than that, because further than that I cannot see. Not yet, anyway. Not yet!"

Chapter Six

It was at the beginning of June that all this happened, which meant that there was less than a month still to pass before the most important time of the year for the village – the time when the men would at last have the chance to make some money out of their fishing.

All winter they had fished every day with lines from small open boats. Yet still their catch never brought more than a bare living to them and their families. Each man of the village, however, was also the owner of a share in another kind of boat – a very much bigger one that was decked in, and that was used for fishing with nets for the great shoals of herring that migrated every summer to northern waters. And there was a big market for herring among the traders who dealt in that kind of fish.

As spring advanced into summer, then, the men had been using all their spare time in making the big boats ready for the whole of the three months they would spend at sea, filling their nets with herring. But they were not the only ones, of course, who were busy with preparations for the start of the herring season, because there was always a great festival held on the day the boats departed for this long absence from their home port. A festival, also, had to have a queen, so that the children of the village school were becoming more and more excited over who would be chosen for this honour: and, to Anna Anderson's great delight that year, it was on her that the choice fell.

"So *you're* to be the Herring Queen!" exclaimed Kristine when Anna came rushing home with the news; and turned from her to look hard at Sarah.

"You're right, Kristine," said Sarah, understanding perfectly what was in that look; and rising from her seat, she went to a drawer she had not opened for well over a year – the drawer that held the strange silk Eric had sent home.

In one move, she had the silk unrolled before them; and there, in their dark little house all cluttered with creels and nets and fishing lines, it was as if she had suddenly spread out the shimmer and gleam of the sea itself. All three of them stood staring in awe at the sight of it, until Sarah said quietly:

"Well, it seems that the Howdy spoke no more than the truth when she said a queen would wear this. Because it would certainly make a far finer dress for the Queen of the Herring Festival than any girl before this has ever worn."

"So the only question now," Kristine exclaimed, "is what kind of dress to make from it!" And immediately, then, the two of them were launched into a great discussion on how they should cut the silk.

Anna, however, was still quite spellbound by the sight of the silk itself; and all she could do was to continue staring at the delicate texture of it, at the silver ripple that ran through its blues and greens, with the colours seeming to shift and move of their own accord from the lightest to the darkest of blue and the lightest to the darkest of green – *the darkest green* . . . Anna jerked suddenly out of her trance as these last words ran through her mind.

"My comb!" she cried; and ran to fetch the comb Eric had sent her. "My green jade comb!"

She placed the comb against the silk, and then looked up to see her mother watching what she had done. Without a word spoken between them, then, Kristine rose and unbraided Anna's long red hair. She swept the whole mass of it to the top of Anna's head, pinned it in place there, and set the comb in it. Then she took the silk and draped it against Anna.

The silk flowed and swirled around her like the flowing and swirling of sea water. The high, curved edge of the green comb rose from her head like a green, glowing crown that not only reflected exactly the dark green of the silk, but that also seemed to make all the other colours flow towards it.

"That's it, then!" Kristine exclaimed. "It's with the comb you'll be crowned on the day of the Festival. And that is how you'll look then."

"But meanwhile," Sarah, suggested, "we'll keep the

business of the dress a secret, eh? Because that way, you see, you'll enjoy yourself even more when you find how much the look of you surprises everybody."

"I'll not say a word," promised Anna, "not even to Jon." And so the making of the dress went on without any but the three of them being aware of it. As it happened, also, it was easy enough to keep the secret from Jon, and from Robert too, both of them being so busy on their own affairs that they were hardly ever in the house.

Robert had work to do at the harbour – because he, too, of course, owned a share in one of the herring boats. He had two shares in this boat, in fact, since the share that had belonged to Eric Anderson was now reckoned to belong to him. What was more, his fellow-fishermen had elected him to take Eric's place as their skipper; and, since the skipper of that particular boat was also the skipper of the whole herring fleet, Robert was extremely proud of having been honoured in this way.

He would do his best, he vowed, to show the men that they were right to have faith in him. And to help matters along in this, he was spending all his spare hours in painting his boat in white, black, and bright blue – these being the colours that fishermen always thought of as the ones that would bring luck to their boats.

As for the way Jon spent his spare time, he was out every day after school with the rest of the village boys, scouring the shore for driftwood to make the huge bonfire that would be lit just before the Herring Festival in honour of St Peter, the patron saint of fishermen. And so the month of June wore on until the dress was ready, with Anna in such excitment over it that she thought about it even in dreams, yet still with the secret of it perfectly kept between her and Kristine and Sarah.

Then came the 29th of June – St Peter's Eve, when all the boats were ready to sail. The church bells were rung, rockets were fired, the bonfire was lit, and Jon had his hour of glory along with the rest of the boys, dancing about in the bonfire's light, throwing potatoes into the flames to be roasted and then daringly raking them out again. But with daylight, of course, it was Anna's turn to shine, because it was on the day following St Peter's Eve that the Herring Festival would be held and the boats would finally depart.

"And a great day it will be for you, too, lass," said Kristine, as she dressed Anna's hair for her; and Sarah added to this, "A day we'll all be proud to remember!"

"Like I'll always be proud of what you've done for me," said Anna, looking down at the shimmering, shifting glory of the dress they had made her. And so, with smiles all round between them, that great day began.

The sun shone brightly for it. There were fiddlers and accordion players to lead the procession that wound its way through the village, and everyone who was fit to walk took part in that procession. The children there were all in their Sunday best. The women wore their traditional fisherwives dress of patterned blouses and skirts in bold stripes of red and black and white.

Kristine had her silver and pearl brooch pinned to her blouse. Sarah wore her white silk shawl over her shoulders. From rooftop to rooftop, there were strings of bunting fluttering in all the colours of the rainbow. The bows of the fiddlers flashed in the sun. The metal mountings of the accordions gleamed. And right behind the fiddlers and the accordion players, came Anna Anderson, The Herring Queen, with the tall lean figure of The Oldest Fisherman proudly stalking alongside, as her escort.

Jimsie was wearing his Sunday suit of navy blue; and in one pocket of his jacket he carried Anna's green jade comb. Anna walked with her left hand resting lightly on Jimsie's right arm; and behind her came the four girl attendants chosen to carry the Queen's gifts to the herring fleet.

One of them held a switch of wood from a rowan tree. Another carried a small velvet cushion with a silver coin resting on it. The third one had a jug of milk, the fourth one carried a small bowl of oatmeal; and like Anna herself, all four of them wore the colours of the sea in dresses made of silk and velvet and silvered fishing nets. But there, as everyone was agreed, the resemblance between Anna and her attendants came to an end.

Those other girls' dresses, certainly, could imitate the colours of the sea; but, as they all turned to tell one another at their very first glimpse of Anna, this one worn by young Anna Anderson was like a living part of the sea itself.

"D'ye see the effect you're having on them?" old Jimsie whispered to her as they walked to the place where he would crown her Queen of the Herring Festival. Anna nodded, her heart dancing with delight in the triumph she was having with her dress.

"It was my granda sent the silk to make the dress," she whispered back to Jimsie; and found herself suddenly wishing with all her heart that Eric could have been there too, to see her being crowned Herring Queen with the green jade comb he had also sent.

They had reached the village square by this time. Jimsie led Anna to stand beside the monument at one side of the square, with her attendants grouped around her. Then, with a wave of his hand that stopped the music, he shouted for silence, and turned to point up to the two figures in the monument. They were the figures of fishermen, one clasping the other in his arms in a way that showed he was trying to drag a drowning man ashore; and with his cracked, but still powerful, voice filling the hush that had now fallen on the square, Jimsie shouted again:

"You know why this is there, all you fathers and mothers. But some of you young ones still need to be told. And so hear me when I tell you now that this monument marks the courage of all those men from our village who daily risk their lives at sea, and the courage also of the women-folk who daily wait and watch for men who may never come home again."

There was not the slightest sound in the square by this time, not even the voice of the smallest child crying. Men and women alike stood with heads bowed, and every man there had taken off his hat as he would take off his hat in church. The powerful voice of The Oldest Fisherman rolled out again over the square; and now, as he shouted, the bowed heads began to lift.

"Yet still we cannot live without the yield of the sea. Out of all that yield, too, nothing is more important to us than the catch of herring that brings the money to see us through the hard days of the winter ahead. And that is why we have a Herring Festival. That is why we have a queen of our Festival to carry out the ceremonies that time has taught us. And so now, as The Oldest Fisherman here, I claim my privilege to crown that queen!"

The people in the square had all begun to smile. Anna looked out over them, proudly smiling in reply; and then was puzzled by her glimpse of Jon's face in the crowd – because Jon was not smiling. He was scowling, in fact; almost, she thought, as if he did not like what he saw when he looked at her. She was not given further time to think about this, however, because Jimsie had taken her green jade comb from his pocket and was holding it high above his head for everyone to see. The next moment he was lowering it towards her head, calling out as he did so:

"Anna Anderson, daughter and granddaughter of fishermen, I crown you Queen of the Herring Festival!"

Anna felt the comb being jammed into the thick mass

of her hair; but the next few moments passed for her in a sort of daze. There was a roar of cheering in the square as the crowd saw the comb glowing like a green crown on the red of her hair. There was music mingling with the roar as the band began blazing out with the tune they called "The Fisherman's Walk". And the next thing she knew, she and Jimsie were moving to the lively time of this tune, with the band marching ahead of them, and the crowd falling in behind as everyone surged down towards the harbour.

It was like being carried along on the crest of some enormous wave, thought Anna as the harbour with its forest of tall brown masts swept by her. She heard shouts as the fisherman dropped from the procession and into the boats. She saw square lug sails beginning to flap against the masts.

"We're nearly there!" Jimsie shouted exultantly, and the next minute they *were* there – right out at the seaward end of one of the long, curving piers of stone that formed the harbour. There waiting her arrival, too, was the leading boat of the fleet – her father's boat. And standing on its deck, only a few feet away from her own place on the pier, was her father, ready to play *his* part in the ceremony.

"Aye, Anna," said Robert, and smiled at her. "You're the bonniest Herring Queen I ever did see."

Anna smiled joyfully back at him. His boat was riding high in the water. *All* the boats were riding high on the tide that was just right to carry them out to sea. As usual, she realised, everything had been timed to exactly the right moment for the fleet's departure.

With a quick wave of her hand, Anna summoned her attendants to her; and one by one, then, she took from them the things they carried. One by one, she offered these to her father, her voice calling clear and loud across the harbour as she did so.

"I give you rowan wood to guard your boats from all harm!"

Robert Anderson leaned forward to take the switch of rowan wood from her, and in an equally clear voice he answered:

"I take the rowan wood to be nailed to the mast of this boat."

Anna reached out the hand holding the silver coin. "I give you silver," she called, "to bring luck to all the nets cast from this fleet."

"I take the silver," Robert answered, "and will throw it into the first of all the nets our boats will cast."

Anna held out both hands, the bowl of oatmeal in one, the jug of milk in the other. "Here," she called, "is food and drink from the land. I give these to you, so that you can share them with the sea."

"I take the food and drink," Robert answered, "and will share these with the sea in return for all it has given us."

Robert turned then, to face the harbour, holding the milk and oatmeal high so that the men in all the other boats could see them. A great cheering shout went up at this, and the shout was followed by a flurry of activity as all the boats cast off from the quayside.

The boats began clearing the harbour, to sail out beyond the pinnacles of The Drongs. Robert's boat reached the open sea beyond The Drongs; and from the crowd on shore came another great cheer as they saw Robert himself standing in the bows of the boat to pour the milk into the water and scatter the oatmeal broadcast on it.

It was not long, then, till the whole prospect of sea from the village was filled with the square sails of the boats, with every eye straining to follow their progress until the very last of the sails had finally vanished over the horizon. There was no time for sadness over this, however, because that was when Jimsie shouted:

"Strike up the band, lads!" And so once more they had cheerful music, with everyone marching in time to it till they reached the field where there would be sports and games for all that was left of the day. And where, of course, the Herring Queen would preside over the games and award all the prizes.

So also would there have been a perfect end to everything that had happened in the great day of Anna Anderson's strange and beautiful sea-dress – if it had not been for one thing. That, unfortunately, was a quarrel that arose between her and her brother Jon. As it happened, too, it was this quarrel that led her to discover the reason behind the scowl she had seen earlier on Jon's face. And even more unfortunately then, it was because

63

of this discovery that the two of them were eventually trapped into the events of the time they were afterwards to call "The Mermaid Summer."

Chapter Seven

The quarrel between Jon and Anna that day, was no more to begin with than an argument over who had come first in one of the races. Anna grew very haughty over this, however, since her judgment as Queen was supposed to be final – so haughty, indeed, that Jon very much resented her manner.

So the argument grew into the kind of quarrel that otherwise very seldom happened between these two; and it was hardly surprising then, that Anna felt this had cast a cloud on what should have been her perfect day. As for Jon, he could not forget his resentment at being ordered about by his younger sister; and so it was not surprising either that the quarrel should go on simmering between them and break out the next day in different form.

Neither of them was at school that day, of course, the school holidays always being timed to start at the beginning of the herring season. But there was still work to be done, in spite of that, just as there was always work for fisher children to do. For a start, there were fish to be caught on the fixed lines that the village boys had to set out every day their fathers were away at the herring; and it was over the work of gathering mussels to bait Jon's line, that the quarrel broke out again.

"We'll get the mussels from the South Rocks," said Anna, thinking that then they would be able to enjoy the company of all the other village children who were in the habit of gathering their mussels from the rocky foreshore lying south of the harbour.

"We will not!" Jon declared. "We'll be far better off working on our own – and anyway, that's not the best place for mussels."

Off he marched then, to the foreshore lying north of the harbour and to the rocks that lay directly opposite to The Drongs. Anna had no choice except to follow him; but she still did not give up her argument, and the more she persisted with this, the more Jon remembered how much he had resented being over-ruled by her on the previous day. His temper began to fray, until finally he turned and shouted at her:

"Now look, Anna, I've had enough of you telling me what to do. Just like I had enough of you yesterday, parading around in that fancy dress of yours!"

"You were just jealous of me, that's all," Anna flared back at him. "*I* saw that look on your face when I was being crowned, and I know now what it meant."

That was when Jon's temper fairly exploded, and it was this explosion of temper that led him into betraying the secret behind the scowling look he had worn then.

"You!" he yelled. "You don't know a thing. I was just

bothered, that's all, because the dress made me remember the time I saw the mermaid!"

Anna gaped at him, too dumbfounded to utter so much as a word. Jon gaped back at her, so dismayed at letting his secret slip out that he could not speak either. Then Anna got her breath back, and questions came pouring from her at such a rate, that Jon realised there was nothing he could do except satisfy her curiosity.

"But you must promise to keep it a secret too," he warned; and once he had got this promise from Anna, he went on to tell her the whole story of his meeting with the mermaid. The one thing he would not tell her, however, was the hiding-place he had found for the conch.

"Because," he said, "I know it's safe where it is. But heaven alone knows what might happen if it's taken out again without good reason; and so I'll not tell *anyone* where it is now."

Now this, of course, was like a challenge to Anna, who took the first chance she had to search for the conch in the one place where she knew that no-one but Jon himself would ever look. This was in the smokehouse, where another part of Jon's work was to keep a basket filled with the oakwood chips her mother and grandmother used for the slowburning fire that was needed to make smoked fish. And sure enough it was there that she found the conch, right at the foot of the basket, and carefully covered over with a great pile of the oakwood chips.

Not a word did she say, however, about this find. Instead, she hid the conch again, but this time under a piece of sacking in the pail she used for gathering mussels. Then, when the two of them were out on the rocks again the following day, she confessed to Jon what she had done, and told him also just why she had done it.

"Because I'm just dying to hear how it sounds," she explained, taking the conch from her pail and holding it out to him. "So will you blow it now for me, Jon? Will you, please?"

"D'you think I'm daft!" Jon exclaimed. "And anyway, what right had you to go poking about in *my* affairs? You'll put that shell back where you found it, my girl, or I'll know the reason why! But I'll not blow it for you – not if you paid me good red gold, I wouldn't!"

"Then I'll blow it myself!" Anna retorted. But that, as she soon found, was a lot easier said than done. Over and over again, she tried to get the right kind of sound from the conch, but still could produce nothing more than the wheezing noises that were all Jon had first got from it. The more she tried and failed, also, the more Jon found himself longing to show off his own skill with the conch; until finally he could no longer resist this feeling.

"Listen," said he, "this is how it should sound." And taking the conch from her, he blew a magnificent blast on it.

Anna laughed with delight at the sound. "Again," she

begged. "Do it again, Jon." And so once again, feeling very proud of his skill, Jon sounded the conch.

"But that's enough," he warned, putting the shell back into the pail. "Remember I've told you that a three-times blast on the conch is a summons to the mermaid."

"I'll remember," Anna agreed. Yet still as she picked up the pail to follow Jon across the rocks, she could not help thinking what fun it would be to have another try at blowing the conch. It wasn't as if she was likely to succeed, after all, she argued to herself, and so it couldn't really do any harm to try. She glanced towards Jon still with his back to her as he walked ahead. Then she put down the pail and reached guiltily for the conch.

She held it then, as she had watched Jon holding it. She blew into it, shaping her lips as she had seen Jon shaping his lips, and the blast she sent out from it this time was a perfect one – a loud and mournful one that came echoing back like the echo of sea sorrow itself. Jon whirled round towards her, fear in his face, anger making his voice hoarse as he shouted:

"That's the third call – the one that makes the three-times summons to the mermaid. And so now you've done it, haven't you?"

But had she? The two of them stood gazing seawards, but nothing strange met their gaze. The sea was blue and unruffled – the same kind of summer sea there had been on the day Jon had first blown the conch. There was no break in its calm except for the white spray bursting always among the pinnacles of The Drongs. There was not the least sight or sound of the mermaid; and Anna grew bold enough at last to suggest:

"Maybe she hasn't heard the conch."

"But maybe she has," Jon retorted. "And if that is so, how can we risk staying to gather mussels?"

But supposing they arrived home empty-handed? That would mean explaining why it was that Jon had no bait for his fishing lines, and then they really would be in trouble!

"So we'll have to get mussels off the South Rocks instead," Anna maintained. "Just as I said we should in the first place."

"And what if she came ashore to us there?" Jon asked. "It would be the whole village then who'd know what we've done, instead of just the family knowing."

For another two or three minutes then, they stood undecided, each of them knowing full well that they could not arrive home empty-handed, each of them knowing equally well the blame that would attach to them if anyone discovered that they had summoned the mermaid.

"If I don't catch fish," Jon said at last, "we don't eat. It's as simple as that. So come on, Anna. We just *have* to take the risk of staying long enough to gather those mussels."

Anna looked doubtfully at him – but how could she refuse her share of the risk when it had been all her fault in the first place? "All right," she agreed, and meekly

70

followed as Jon set out for the edge of the rocks where he was sure he would find the best mussels – the ones that grew big and fat from being washed regularly by the tide.

There didn't seem to be much of a risk to this, either, as it happened, because a full half hour went by with nothing at all to bother them except an occasional stumble on a slippery part of the rocks. Jon worked steadily at cutting the mussels free with the sharp, curved blade of his knife. Anna followed behind him, working just as steadily at scooping the mussels into her bucket.

They had this bucket nearly full, in fact, before the risk finally became reality. Jon was straightening up from cutting free a last clump of mussels, Anna was bending to pick up the clump, when the mermaid's head broke through the surface of the water and they both found themselves staring straight into her eyes.

For a long moment, neither of them moved – neither of them *could* move, in fact, so deeply were they frozen with shock and fear. The mermaid opened her mouth to speak, and Jon knew without being told that she was once again going to ask why he had summoned her. Despairingly, he cast around for some excuse that might divert her anger from him; but just at the very moment the mermaid would have spoken, Anna broke from her frozen trance and stepped uncertainly back from the water's edge.

The mermaid's eyes followed the movement. Her gaze rested on Anna's skirt, and the legs showing beneath it; and with a look of great curiosity coming into her face, she exclaimed:

"It's a female land creature. And it's got legs!"

There was nothing the mermaid could have said that would have been a greater surprise to Jon and Anna at that moment; and strangely enough, this feeling of surprise had the effect of releasing them – for the time being, at least – from their fear.

"Of course I have legs!" Anna exclaimed. "Why shouldn't I have legs? And why should that surprise you?"

"Why should it not?" the mermaid countered. "I have seen men before this; often and often I have seen them, because men are fishers and sailors. And so I know that they have legs. As for the young of men – creatures like that one beside you – I know that they also have legs, because they too often go to sea. But I have never before seen a female of your kind, because they are neither fishers nor sailors; and so how was I to know that they, too, have legs?"

She was beginning to get angry, Jon thought; and indeed, he was right in this, because the mermaid had given a great swish of her tail as she asked her last question. It was this very question, all the same, that gave him the idea for an excuse for summoning her; and quickly then he exclaimed:

"But that was just why I summoned you! So that you *could* have a chance to see this – er – this female person." The mermaid gave another swish of her tail, but a gentler one this time, and looked again at Anna's legs.

"It must be strange," she said thoughtfully, "to move about on such things."

Anna smiled at this remark. Anna, in fact was beginning to enjoy her encounter with the mermaid. "I was thinking the same about your tail," she confessed. "And something else I was thinking. They say you're old – and you must be, because you've lived for so long in this sea. But you don't look old. You look very young, in fact; not much older than I am myself. And you're beautiful."

Anna gave another smile, an admiring one, as she said this. The mermaid smiled back at her, and Anna could not help adding then, "*Very* beautiful!"

The mermaid dived suddenly, her great tail lifting high above the water in a blinding sparkle of scales. Then just as suddenly, she surfaced again – as if, it occurred to Jon, she had performed the whole movement for joy of what Anna had just said to her. The next moment, also, Jon found he had been right in thinking this, because the next moment the mermaid was saying to Anna:

"I have sister mermaids, and I can see that they are beautiful. But I cannot tell what I am like, because I have never seen myself except, very dimly, in the waters of the sea. And no one has ever said to me that *I* am beautiful."

"Oh, but you are!" Anna exclaimed. "Your skin is the colour of the pearl in my mother's brooch, and it has the same gleam as that pearl. And your eyes – there is only one thing I know of that is the colour of your eyes. Look! I'll show it to you."

Quickly she thrust a hand into the pocket of her dress, remembering that she had brought her green comb with her to use if her hair fell over her eyes while she was bending to gather mussels. She drew the comb from her pocket, held it so that the mermaid could see it clearly, and said:

"There now! You see how the dark green of it glows? It's made of jade, my mother says, and your eyes have just the glow and colour of jade."

"Jade . . ." Softly, as if speaking to herself, the mermaid murmured the word, and watched as Anna pinned the comb into her hair. In a louder tone, then, the mermaid said, "There is no such thing in the sea as jade." Her stare at the comb took on a strangely fixed look; then suddenly, and still without taking her eyes off it, she exclaimed:

"I want it! Give it to me!"

Her voice, till then, had been a soft and pleasant one. Now it was harsh, and there was such menace in it, that both Jon and Anna shrank back from her.

"Give it to me!" she repeated; and with panic beginning to rise in him, Jon nudged Anna and whispered:

"Go on! Give it to her!"

"No!" Anna exclaimed. "That's my Granda's present to me, and I won't give it to anyone."

The mermaid's eyes flashed iwth rage. She raised her

tail and brought it down with an angry slap that sent water spraying into Anna's face.

"I want it!" she screamed; and now her face was not at all beautiful. It was not young, either, but old with an unguessable age, and instead of a pearly glow, it now had the sick-looking paleness of a dead fish's belly. "I want it!" she screamed again. "Give it to me! Give it to me!"

"No, no, *no*!" Anna shouted back at her. She was trembling with fear by then; but in spite of her fear, she too was now angry at the very thought of being made to give up the comb. Out of all the presents her grandfather had sent her, after all, it was the one she valued most; and so now she snatched it out of her hair, held tightly to it, and shouted again at the mermaid:

"It's mine – d'you hear? And I shall never, never give it to you."

Anna turned, on this shout of defiance, and began running away across the rocks. Jon followed her; and following after both of them came the screaming sound of the mermaid's voice:

"But I shall make you give it up! Just wait till you see what I will do to your herring fleet, and you will be glad then to let me have it!"

Chapter Eight

The mermaid's threat against the herring fleet was something that Anna had not bargained on when she refused to give up the comb. Neither had Jon, of course, and they were both very worried about it. To make things worse, too, they knew that they would be the guilty ones if anything did happen – Jon for having summoned the mermaid in the first place, and Anna for having angered her into making the threat.

"You'll *have* to give her the comb," Jon kept insisting; but this continued to be the one thing that Anna would not agree to do. It was not only because she was so fond of the comb, either; nor was it entirely because she valued it so much as a present from her Granda Eric. Ever since The Oldest Fisherman had crowned her with the comb, in fact, Anna had felt it to be more than ever a link between her grandfather and herself. And if she gave up the comb, it seemed to her, that link would be broken and she really would never see him again.

"But Jon," she argued, "I can't give it to her now unless you summon her again. And you don't want to do that, do you? Besides which, we don't know if she *can* do anything against the herring fleet."

No, Jon admitted, he did *not* want to summon her again; and so, he finally agreed with Anna, the best thing to do before taking any decision on this, would be to wait till they had some definite news of the fleet.

There would be no problem, either, in gathering this news, because the way of things in the herring season was that boats went out from every village along that coast. The nightly catch from all these boats, too, had to be brought ashore as quickly as possible, or else it would spoil; and so, all along that coast also, there would be men coming ashore from the herring boats of those other villages, all of them with news of what was happening to other boats on other parts of the coast.

"But *I* can't be the one to hang around the harbour all day listening for news," Jon pointed out, "because you know I've promised to spend all my spare time in the holidays helping out at the boatyard. And you know, too, how much I've set my heart on an apprenticeship there."

That was true, Anna agreed. And if Jon broke that promise, there certainly wouldn't be much chance of the boatbuilder taking him on as an apprentice. But it was true also, that there was nothing to stop her being at the harbour every day, because her work in the holidays was the same as that of her mother and her grand-mother. She had to knit socks and stockings and shawls for sale in the town, just as they did; and knitting was work that could be done anywhere.

"Besides which," she told Jon, "*I* don't mind sitting on the harbour wall all day, – not so long as I've got old Jimsie to talk to."

So for the next two weeks Anna was out in the sunshine of that summer, sitting alongside old Jimsie Jamieson on the harbour wall, her hands busy with her knitting as she chatted to him and to the various fisher-men who came ashore after the herring had been unloaded from their boats. By the end of that time, also, she had some disturbing news for Jon.

"There's something strange happening to the boats from our village," she told him. "All the boats that have fished alongside them have had good catches. But with our boats, it seems, they only have to appear for the herring to vanish – almost as if something had chased them away, I heard one man telling old Jimsie. Which means they've had hardly any fish so far."

"H'mph!" said Jon. "So much for throwing silver into the nets to bring them luck – because how can they have luck in catching fish when there's none left for them to catch? And if that's because something is chasing the herring away from the nets, it's not hard to guess that the something is the mermaid. So you'll have to give her the comb after all, Anna. You'll just have to."

"I won't, I won't!" cried Anna, stubborn as ever on this point.

"Then you'll go hungry this winter, the same as the

rest of the family will," Jon shouted at her. "Be reasonable, girl. You know we can't live through a winter unless we've had a good herring season."

It was no good appealing to Anna's reason on this, however – not so long as she was convinced that parting with the comb meant parting for ever, also, with her Granda Eric. And so another week went by, with still no better news of their boats. Anna was having some uneasy nights by this time, nights that were haunted by dreams of the mermaid – strange dreams in which she saw the mermaid once again reaching out a hand towards her comb and once again screaming:

"*Give it to me! I want it, I want it!*"

Then came one night when Anna awoke with a great start to hear the sound of singing. It was a single voice that sang, piercingly sweet, and very softly. Yet the voice was nowhere in the room; and to Anna it seemed that she was hearing it the way you can hear a sound from a shell when you hold it close up against your ear.

It flashed through Anna's mind that it must be the mermaid she could hear; and immediately then, she began shaking Jon awake. He grunted crossly, sat up in bed and listened; but Jon, it seemed, could hear nothing; and even more crossly he told her:

"Go back to sleep, Anna. You've been dreaming again, that's all." Within seconds then, in spite of all Anna's persuasions, he himself was as deeply asleep as ever, leaving Anna trying to decide what to do next. Should she wake her mother? Her grandmother? That would mean confessing she had been guilty of turning the mermaid's anger against the herring fleet – and anyway, would they hear the voice any more than Jon had?

In fearful wonder she stood listening to the voice still going on and on in her ear; a voice, she was beginning to accept, that was meant for her alone. There were no words in the song it sang; and yet still the music of it was creating one picture after another in her mind. There was the sea in these pictures, and the movement of the sea. The sea had long, silk-smooth waves. The waves rolled gently, so gently that she felt a great longing to lie down on their silken smoothness and be rocked back to sleep, back to sleep. . . .

The longing drew Anna towards the door of the house, the door beyond which she would find the sea. She opened the door, and stepped outside. The moon was at its full, that night, lighting the dark clutter of masts in the harbour, spreading silver on the sea beyond the boats lying at anchor there. Like a sleepwalker, Anna began moving in the direction the voice seemed to urge her to move – towards the rocks stretching darkly away from the harbour's northern wall.

She reached the shoreward edge of the rocks, and with every step she took towards this point, the less it seemed that the voice was sounding close in her ear and the more it seemed to be coming from the seaward edge of these rocks. It was louder too, now. The call it was sending out to her was becoming more and more urgent.

The sea visions it bred in her mind were ever more enticing.

Bare-footed, just as she had left the house, Anna began crossing the rocks. Seaweed tripped her, the sharp edges of shells and the rough surface of the rocks cut and bruised her feet; but reaching the promise the voice held out to her was all she cared about, and she did not notice these things. Closer she drew to the seaward edge of the rocks, closer to the waves rolling gently there, the long silken waves that would soothe her, caress her, if she laid herself down on them.

She reached the very edge of the rocks, paused there for a moment; then, with a sigh of sheer pleasure was just about to let herself slide forward on to the smoothness of the waves when there was a sudden end to the sea-song that had tempted her. On the instant, then, she was awake from her trance, and realising with horror that she had been just about to drown herself. Trembling all over, she stepped back from the edge of the rocks, and saw that the mermaid was sitting there, right beside her.

Anna would have bolted straight for home at that moment, if she had not been so shaken by her experience. As it was, all she could do was stand there trying to control her trembling while the mermaid said:

"Well, now you have seen how easily I can bring you to me. And so, are you ready yet to give me that comb I want from you?"

She was leaning back on her hands as she spoke, her tail swishing idly in the water, her head tilted to look up at Anna. There were strands of pearls twisted through the long hair streaming down from her back-tilted head, a golden comb set on top of it, and around her neck there were more pearls – rope after rope of pearls clustering white and gleaming against the gleaming whiteness of her skin. She looked so sure of herself too, posed like this in all the magnificence of her sea-array, that Anna felt annoyance at her beginning to take over from the first shock of fear at seeing her there.

"You nearly drowned me!" she accused; but the mermaid only smiled at this and agreed:

"That's true. But I stopped my song in time, didn't I? Because if I *had* drowned you, I never would have got the comb. Would I? But now you must agree to give it to me, because now also, I have done as I threatened I would do. I have chased all the herring away from the boats of your fleet – as you must know by this time, I am sure, because gossip always travels fast among the fishing boats."

"Yes," Anna told her, "I do know that. And you, I suppose, do not care at all that we shall go hungry this winter because of it."

"Why should I care?" the mermaid asked. "I have never known what it feels like to go hungry; and so long as there are fish in the sea, I never shall."

"But why *should* you want the comb so much?" cried Anna, and threw out a hand despairingly to the splendour of the mermaid's pearls and gold. "You have string upon string of pearls there, and a golden comb besides.

And so why should *my* comb matter so much to you?

"Pearls!" the mermaid said scornfully. "A golden comb! I have worn these tonight only to let you see that I can have such things at any time I please. Just as my sister mermaids can, too. They can dive for pearls, as I do. They can find golden combs in the treasure from wrecked ships, just as I have. But none of us has ever seen the like of your comb, and that is why I must have it."

"But I'll not give it to you," Anna insisted stubbornly, "and so you will just have to be content with what you do have."

"Would you still say that," the mermaid asked, "if I threatened to bring you here again, and to make it part of the spell that you should wear the comb when you came? Because then, you see, I would not stop my song before you drowned. And once you *were* drowned, I would take the comb from you and make it mine."

"You would not," Anna retorted, "because now I shall give my comb to a friend to keep for me. And so, if you *do* cast your spell on me again, I will not be able to bring it with me."

"But do you not see," the mermaid cried, "that my sisters have everything that *I* have? And so, if I have that comb, they will all be jealous of me. Because you told me, did you not, that it exactly matches the colour of my eyes. And none of them will be able to say that about *their* combs, so that I shall be grander than any of them."

Now Anna, all the time the mermaid had been

making this speech, had been thinking hard. The mermaid was vain, she had realised, most terribly vain; and so, if there was to be any way at all of outwitting the creature, it would have to be by playing on this vanity.

"Listen," said she, crouching down so that she could speak face to face with the mermaid, "if you want to make your sisters *really* jealous of you, I can give you something that would let you have an even greater victory in than that you would have with my comb."

The mermaid looked suspiciously at her; and then, with a swish of her tail that was meant to warn Anna not to trifle with her, she asked, "And what, pray, might that be?"

"You'll see," Anna promised. "You'll see. But first of all, you'll have to make a bargain with me. You've taken three weeks good fishing away from our herring fleet; and so, for the next three weeks, you must make sure that all our boats make heavy catches of fish. You must make all their losses up to them, in fact, before I bring you this other thing. And if you do not do that, I will never bring it to you at all, and so you will never know what you have missed. Isn't that so?"

The mermaid gave her another long look, but this time there was more of greed in it, than suspicion; and Anna realised she had been greatly tempted by the offer of this mysterious "something" that would make her sister mermaids really jealous of her.

"You speak of weeks," the mermaid said abruptly,

"but mermaids do not measure time like that. How long is a week?"

Anna looked up to the full moon gently gliding like a pale bride in the sky. "When the moon has reached its last quarter," she said, "three weeks will have passed. And that is when I will summon you again, to give you what I have to give. But only, remember, if you have made good by then the losses our fleet has suffered. Is it agreed?"

"Agreed," the mermaid said; and in one single, graceful movement then, she had slid off the rocks and was back in the water. Without sound or splash she disappeared beneath it, and Anna was left alone looking out over the moon's bridal trail lying silver over the sea, and wondering how difficult it might be to get Jon to agree to the plan she had in mind.

Chapter Nine

There was no chance for Anna to speak privately to Jon on the day after her moonlight meeting with the mermaid. Her bare feet had been so badly bruised and cut by the rocks on that occasion, that she could hardly bear to put them to the ground; and so, while he went out and about as usual, she had to stay indoors.

"Although what you've been doing to get your feet in such a state," scolded Kristine as she bandaged the cuts, "is more than any reasonable Christian body could imagine."

"I was sleepwalking," said Anna, getting as near the truth as she could without betraying what had really happened.

"God save us!" cried Kristine. "And with the harbour so near, too! It's a mercy of heaven, girl, that you weren't drowned."

"That's true," agreed Anna, shivering as she thought how nearly that had happened, and feeling all the more anxious for the chance of a secret talk with Jon.

The minute she was able to hobble out of doors, then,

she seized the first chance that offered to tell him all about her meeting with the mermaid. Jon listened, with dismay growing on his face all the time she spoke; and as soon as she had finished telling him about the plan she had formed, he exclaimed:

"I'll have nothing to do with that, Anna. It could be dangerous for you – just too dangerous."

"I know that," Anna told him. "But it was still the only way I could think of to buy time, Jon. And *that's* what we need now – time to let the herring fleet make up the losses it's suffered."

"Maybe so," Jon admitted. "But what will happen, Anna, once we come to the end of the three weeks time you've bought? Because I tell you now, I don't believe this plan of yours will work, and I just don't understand why you believe it *should* work."

"I can see you don't," Anna told him. "But that's because you're a boy and so you don't understand how the mermaid thinks."

Jon laughed at this. "And you do, I suppose," he jeered.

"Yes, I do." Anna retorted. "Or at least, I think I do, because I'm a girl and she's a woman – or half a woman, anyway. And so I've got at least half a chance of being right, haven't I?"

Jon thought for a bit about this. Whether Anna was right or not, he realised, she had still made a promise to the mermaid. And so, if she failed to carry out that promise, the creature was bound to be even more angry than ever. And there was no telling what might happen then!

"All right," he said at last. "I still don't like it, Anna. I still don't believe it will work. But I can't see any way out of that promise you've made, and so I'll do as you ask. When the time comes, I'll summon her for you. *And* I'll do my best to protect you against the danger from her."

"Good!" exclaimed Anna, feeling most relieved at this final assurance. But she still had to make sure that the mermaid would never be able to tempt her out while she was wearing her green comb; and so, while Jon went off to the boatyard, she hobbled down to the harbour to see The Oldest Fisherman.

"I want you to keep this safe for me," she told him, fetching the comb from the pocket of her dress as she spoke. "And I want you, too, to promise that you'll never, never tell anyone that you have it."

Jimsie's bushy eyebrows shot up in surprise. "Now why," he asked, "would you need me to do that for you?"

"I can't tell you," Anna said. "I can't tell anyone, Jimsie."

"Now wait a minute, Anna," Jimsie exclaimed, looking keenly at her. "Are you in trouble of some kind?"

"I am," admitted Anna, "and so is Jon. And I'll be in even worse trouble if you *don't* keep the comb for me."

Jimsie stroked his beard and thought for a minute. "Well, if it's like that," he said at last, "I'll do what you ask. But on one condition, Anna. If this trouble gets to be too much for you and Jon to handle on your own, you must tell me about it. Will you promise me that in return for my promise to keep the comb safe and never tell a soul I have it?"

This struck Anna as being a fair enough bargain, even though it seemed to her that there was no chance of either Jimsie or anyone else being able to help with the problem of the mermaid. So it was with that she gave Jimsie the comb along with the promise he had asked for; after which there was nothing else she could do except to wait for news of what might happen during the rest of the three weeks time she had won for the fishing-fleet.

The rest of the first week passed. Her wounded feet were almost healed by then – quick healing always being the way with young people – and she could walk easily every day down to the harbour. The second week went by, and by the end of that week there was boat after boat coming in with gossip about the extraordinary change of luck that had happened to the boats from their own village.

By the end of the third week, the gossip had become firm news in the form of a letter from Robert telling them exactly what was happening to the village boats. They were having such huge catches of herring every night, he wrote, that all their previous losses had now been made good; and if matters continued in the same way, there was no doubt that it would be the best herring season they had ever had.

"So it looks as if there's every chance now of us all being safe for the winter ahead," Sarah and Kristine told one another happily. But Jon and Anna, of course, could not share their joy in this, even although they too were relieved to know that there would be no lean and hungry times for them that winter.

All *they* could think of, in fact, was the price they had still to pay for the good news that had made everyone else so happy. And supposing the mermaid was not satisfied with that price? Supposing Anna's plan did *not* work? With dread filling his mind, Jon put these questions to himself, while even Anna gradually became more and more afraid of the moment when she would have to put her plan to the test.

Each one of them, however, had the sense not to mention such fears to the other, and when the time came to carry out the plan, Jon put on as bold a face as he could.

"Right, then, Anna," he said, and Anna was relieved to see how confident he looked. "The three weeks are up now. Get the pail for the mussels. I'll get my conch, and we'll go out to meet the mermaid."

So once again in bright sunlight the two of them clambered over the rocks till they reached the loneliest and farthest out part of them – the part that lay nearest to the ugly pinnacles of The Drongs. There, Jon took his conch out from under his gansey, and blew the summons to the mermaid. There also, Anna unwrapped the bundle she had made of her Herring Queen dress.

Jon moved away from her and began, as usual, to gather mussels for his fishing lines. Anna slipped off the dress she was wearing. She put on the Herring Queen dress instead, and stood watching the water between herself and The Drongs. For long minutes she stood there, the sun striking off the silk of the dress and making her seem like a glittering, gleaming pillar of colour rising from the rocks. For long minutes, nothing happened. Then suddenly, out at The Drongs, there was a flash of silver.

"Jon!" Anna called. "She's coming!" Jon hurried to her side, and as they stood there together, Anna said quietly, "I'm frightened, Jon." Jon answered her, speaking as quietly as she had.

"So am I, Anna." Anna looked at him in dismay. If her big brother was frightened too, she asked herself, what hope was there for either of them now? Jon caught her look and gave a grim little smile in reply to it. "But don't worry, Anna," he added. "I'll still do my best to look after you."

There was a swirl of movement in the water beside the rocks. The mermaid surfaced out of the swirl, grasped the edge of the rocks, and hung there, staring upwards. But it was only towards Anna that she stared, quite ignoring Jon, and letting her gaze travel, instead, over the glittering spectacle of Anna's Herring Queen dress. Wider and wider grew her eyes as they took in every detail of it; but not a word did she say, and it was Anna, eventually, who was the first to speak.

"Well?" she asked. "Do you like the dress?"

"I've never seen *anything* so beautiful!" the mermaid exclaimed. "It has the colours of the sea in it, the movement of the sea, all the moods of the sea! And the colours gleam too, the way they do in my own tail!" A shiver of delight ran over her as she spoke these final words. She smiled, and with an answering smile Anna told her:

"Yes, indeed, it's beautiful enough for a queen to wear. So now you see that I've kept my side of the bargain we made, just as you've kept your side of it. Because I promised you something wonderful, didn't I? And here it is now, this dress, with me wearing it just to let you really see how wonderful it is."

Another shiver of delight ran over the mermaid – an even stronger one that finished with her suddenly making the same kind of dive she had performed to show her pleasure on the occasion Anna had told her that *she* was beautiful.

"You see?" Anna whispered turning quickly to Jon as the mermaid dived, "I was right, wasn't I? I *told* you she wouldn't be able to resist it!" The mermaid surfaced. Smiling, she grasped the edge of the rocks and looked up towards Anna.

"You were right!" she exclaimed. "I will have a famous victory with that dress. Give it to me!"

She reached up towards the dress, water dripping from her slim, shining arm and long white fingers. The fingers grasped a handful of the silk. The water dripping from them made a trail of damp that dimmed the silk's bright colours; and immediately she saw this happen, the mermaid snatched back her hand. Anger glared in her eyes. She gave a tremendous flip of her tail that sent water showering all over Anna.

The water soaked the silk of the dress and left it clinging to her with all its colour quite blotted out by the damp, and all its gleaming glory gone. With dismay, she looked at it then; and accusingly as she looked, the mermaid cried:

"So this is your wonderful something – a dress that is coloured like the sea, but has no colour at all once the sea touches it! And my sisters would be jealous of me having that, would they?" Angrily she lashed again at the water with her tail, and viciously again demanded, "Would they?"

Jon gripped Anna by the elbow, alarm at the mermaid's tone making him ready to take her running away with him. Anna stood staring at the mermaid herself, not knowing in the least what to say to soothe her anger; and all the time she stood helpless like this, the mermaid raged on.

"You have tricked me!" she screamed. "And in more ways than one, too. You have tried to enchant me with the look the dress had before the sea took back from it the beauty of its sea-colours. But even if that had not been so, what is the use of my having a dress when I cannot walk about in it as you do? And do you think my sisters would not have realised that and laughed at me for it?

But I am not the fool you have taken me to be – oh, no, I am not, and now—"

"Wait, oh wait, please," Anna interrupted, suddenly finding her voice again in a desperate cry of pleading. "I didn't think – I mean I didn't realise it would be like this. Honestly, I didn't. The dress *is* so beautiful, you see, far more beautiful than anyone has ever seen before. And the colours of it *are* so much sea-colours, the gleam of them *is* so much the gleam of your own tail, that I was sure you would really want to have it. And you did, too, – didn't you?"

"You know I did," the mermaid retorted. "But that was only at first, before I saw how the sea would change it, and how useless it would be to me anyway. And so now you must take the consequences for failing to keep your side of the bargain – or else you must do as I wanted in the first place and give me that green comb."

"And if I don't?" Anna asked.

"I'll do as I did before," the mermaid told her. "I'll chase the herring away from your boats."

Jon gave Anna a nudge at this, a very warning nudge that was clearly intended to make her agree at last to giving up the comb. Anna nodded, to let him see that she understood what was in his mind. But even so, she was now also thinking hard of some way to avoid this, just as hard as she had thought on the previous occasion she had talked to the mermaid. She was remembering, too, just how vain the mermaid was; and so now she said:

"It would be a shame if you did that when I could

bring you something you would find even more wonderful than the dress."

The mermaid looked suspiciously at her. "Maybe," she retorted. "But I don't trust you."

"That's not fair," Anna protested. "I admit I made a mistake about the dress. But I wasn't trying to trick you. And this other something I could bring you will *not* spoil in the sea. What's more, it will bring you the greatest pleasure you could ever possibly have."

The mermaid hesitated, swishing her long tail thoughtfully back and forward. She frowned, and then asked abruptly, "Is it beautiful, this something?"

"It is," Anna told her. Then, looking straight into the mermaid's eyes, and choosing her words very carefully, she added, "It is exactly as beautiful as you are."

"Impossible!" the mermaid cried. "How can anything be exactly as beautiful as anything else."

"I'll prove it to you," Anna told her, "if you give me the chance. Just let me have the same three weeks as you did before. Promise not to interfere with our boats for that three weeks, and at the end of them, I will bring you this something."

"Do *you* promise?" the mermaid asked.

"I do," said Anna. "And I promise, too, that you will find everything I have told you about it is true. Is it a bargain?"

"A bargain," the mermaid agreed. "But it will be the worse for you, I warn you, if you do not keep strictly to your side of it."

As quickly as always, then, she dived out of sight. Jon and Anna stood in silence for a few moments after that; but as soon as he was sure she had indeed gone, Jon turned to Anna and let out all the rage he had felt at having to keep silent while she made this extraordinary bargain with the mermaid.

"You'll never be able to keep such a bargain," he shouted. "Never! Never!"

"Yes, I will," Anna insisted. And while they walked home she explained to him just how she intended to manage that.

Chapter Ten

The further three weeks that Anna had won from the mermaid went past with news of the herring fleet having such continued success that everyone in the village was happy – except, that is, for Jon and Anna. They were far too well aware that, once again, they would have to pay the price for all that good fishing; and even although Anna had managed to convince Jon that she could indeed keep her bargain with the mermaid, they were both still nervous of the moment when she would have to prove this.

As time went on, too, they began to find that keeping the whole business so secret was becoming more and more of a strain on both of them. As for Jon, he continued to be so worried at the danger Anna was courting, that over and over again he came back to the idea that she should give up the comb to the mermaid and so let them be done for good and all with the whole business.

The very thought of giving up the comb, however, was still too much for Anna; and so, altogether, it was a miserable state of affairs for both of them till the moment finally came for summoning the mermaid again. With Anna standing close beside him, then, Jon sent out his three blasts on the conch; and this time there was no delay in the mermaid's response to the summons.

Within seconds of its sound dying away, she had surfaced beside them, her face streaming water, her hands with their coral-pink nails eagerly grasping the edge of the rock. And no sooner was she there than she was demanding of Anna:

"Well, where is it? Where is this wonderful thing that is exactly as beautiful as I am?"

Carefully Anna unwrapped the cloth she had used to bundle up her Granda Eric's present of the silver hand-mirror. It was just the way she had always kept it, the glass clean, the frame and the handle brightly polished. The glass sparkled in the summer sun of that day. The silver of the handle shone. The flower petals that made the silver frame caught the sun in a thousand glittering points of light.

It was such a perfectly lovely thing, indeed, that Anna felt a dreadful pang at the thought of parting with it. But she had to, of course, because the whole purpose of her plan was to play on the great vanity of the mermaid. In silence, she held out the mirror, handle foremost. The mermaid grasped the handle, looked in the glass, and saw her own face reflected at the heart of the flower made by its silver-petalled frame. For a long moment she stared at the reflection, her green eyes wide, a look of awe on the pearl-like paleness of her face. Then she spoke, in a voice that was barely above a whisper.

"I'm beautiful," the whisper said. "Oh! *I am so beautiful!*"

"Yes," said Anna soberly. "You are. But you'd never seen yourself clearly before – you told me that, remember? And so you didn't know till now just how beautiful you are. Did you?"

The mermaid shook her head, still staring at herself in the mirror. She smiled, then laughed aloud as she saw the reflection smiling back at her. Anna glanced at Jon, and he gave her an encouraging little nod. The plan was working, that nod said; and so boldly she went on:

"Well, then, you can see now too that I've kept at least one part of the promise I made you. Because it's only your own reflection that could be exactly as beautiful as you are. Isn't that so?"

The mermaid glanced up from the mirror, her smile fading, suspicion beginning to darken the green of her eyes. Slowly she said, "You are very cunning. Because that is something I cannot deny. But you have something else yet to prove, because you also promised that this thing would not be spoilt by the sea the way the dress was spoiled."

"And it won't," Anna assured her. "Just try it and see."

The words were hardly out of her mouth before the mermaid gave a backward flip that took her out of sight under the water. She surfaced again, the mirror held high in one hand, with water streaming off its gleaming surface. With her free hand grasping the rock, she held it in front of her, and saw her face reflected in it as clearly as she had seen it before. Her suspicion vanished. Once again, she smiled, admiring the effect of this in the mirror as she did so.

"You spoke the truth," she told Anna. "The sea cannot damage *this*! And, oh, how jealous all my sisters will be when I show it to them!"

"Well, then!" Anna exclaimed, "there is all of my promise now fulfilled – because what *could* give you greater pleasure than to make your sisters jealous?"

The mermaid gave her a sly, sideways glance. "Nothing at all," she said, and laughed softly at her own words. "There is nothing would please me more than to see their faces twist with envy over this. And so, yes indeed, you have kept every word of your side of our bargain."

Anna gave a great sigh of relief, and so did Jon. "Then it's all over," Anna said thankfully, and smiled at the mermaid. "You'll take the mirror instead of the comb."

"Oh, yes," the mermaid told her. "I'll take the mirror. But not *instead* of the comb."

"But I've kept every word of my side of our bargain!" Anna cried. "You've just this moment admitted that!"

"So I have," the mermaid agreed. "And *I* have kept my side of the bargain too. All these three weeks past, I have not interfered with the boats at the herring fishing. But there was nothing at all in our bargain about the green comb. And so you must still give it to me, because I still want it. *And I will have it!*"

Her eyes grew dark and angry again as she spoke these last words; and, as always when she was angry, she lashed the water with her tail. Both Jon and Anna drew back a step from her. Then, very uncertainly, Anna once again asked:

"And – and if I don't give it to you?"

"I'll drown every man aboard the boats of your herring fleet," the mermaid told her. There was no mistaking either, that she meant what she said; but even so, Jon could not help crying out then:

"I don't believe you! You couldn't raise a storm that would wreck all our boats! I don't believe that even you could do that!"

"Neither do I," Anna chimed in. "And besides, we have done things that will protect the boats against storms. We have given food and drink to the sea in return for all it has given us. There is rowan wood nailed to the mast of my father's boat, and rowan is a strong charm against bad luck. We—"

"Enough!" the mermaid interrupted angrily. "I never said I would raise the sea against the boats. I said I would *drown the men!*"

Jon and Anna looked in horror at her, both of them immediately remembering the time she had almost succeeded in drowning their father and grandfather along with all their crew, and the way she had done *that*. The mermaid guessed from their faces that they had understood at last what she meant; and grimly she told them:

"Yes, I shall draw them to me with my singing. And there is not one man will escape alive from the wild waters around the rocks where I shall sit in wait to send out my song to them."

There was a long silence. Jon and Anna stood staring at one another in this silence. The mermaid continued to admire herself in the mirror.

"You'll *have* to give it to her," Jon whispered at last.

"I know," Anna whispered in reply. But even so, she was still stubborn enough to make one last fight against this final, terrible threat.

"I'll give you the comb," she told the mermaid, "provided that you give our fleet yet another three weeks to allow them to finish the herring season."

"No!" the mermaid shouted. "I want that comb, and I want it quickly. Three days is the most I'll give you. And if you are not here with it in exactly three days from now, you will never see any man of that fleet again."

With a final glare of anger, then, she dived out of sight. Jon and Anna were left watching the ripples of her dive, before they turned for home, with Anna sadly at last accepting the loss of her comb, and Jon trying to tell her that it wouldn't really be so bad not to have it.

"Although I still don't see," he said, "why you wouldn't give it to her in the first place, and so have saved us all this trouble we've had."

"That's because you don't understand about Granda

Eric," Anna told him, trying not to cry as she thought that now she never would see her Granda Eric again. "So long as I had that comb, you see, I had the feeling he would come back home some day."

"Well, maybe he will yet, even without the comb," said Jon, trying to comfort her; but Anna was so far from any kind of comfort on this that her tears finally began to flow in good earnest. By the time they reached the harbour, too, she was still sniffling. And when the two of them stopped there so that she could ask Jimsie Jamieson to give the comb back to her, it was no use trying to pretend to him that there was nothing wrong.

"I'll give you back your comb, Anna," said Jimsie, "but don't forget you made a promise in return for the safe-keeping I've given it. You said you'd tell me if the trouble you and Jon are having became too much for you to handle. Didn't you, now?"

"We can still handle it," Jon said quickly; and with a warning glance at Anna, he added, "Can't we, Anna?"

"Yes," Anna agreed, "but all the same, Jon—" She hesitated, once again thinking hard. Was it possible that Jimsie *could* help them? She hadn't thought so before, of course; but matters were so desperate now that she was willing to take any chance at all of being able to keep her comb – and so of seeing her Granda Eric again. Jon began to tug at her arm, urging her away with him; but there was nobody could make Anna Anderson do anything against her will, and it was Jon's very eagerness to get her away that finally decided her.

"I'm going to tell Jimsie," she said, breaking away from Jon's hold on her; and before he could say a word to stop her, she was pouring out the whole story of that mermaid summer. Jimsie listened with all sorts of expressions chasing one another over his bearded old face – surprise at first, then fear, then interest, and also admiration for the way Anna had held off the mermaid's demands, and so gained time for the herring fleet to make good catches.

"Sit down," he told her and Jon when she came to the end of the story. "Sit here beside me and let me think."

Anna sat down on the harbour wall. Jon sat beside her, scowling, and muttering that now everyone in the village would know what had been going on, and what would they have to say to that? Jimsie began working again on the piece of green serpentine he had been carving. Anna watched his hands, and tried to pretend she couldn't hear Jon's angry muttering. The figure Jimsie was carving was that of a mermaid; and after he had worked on this for a few minutes he said:

"Well now, let the blame for what you've told me lie where it may, there's one question that stands out from it all. What will happen if Anna *does* hand over the comb?"

There was a moment's silence, with Jon and Anna both wondering why Jimsie had asked this question. Jimsie went on with his carving, and then looked up again to say:

"All right, then, I'll tell you. That mermaid has

discovered the power of what they call "blackmail" – which means threatening that something terrible will happen if what she wants is not given to her. Now, do you think for one moment that she'll stop using that power even after she does get the comb?"

This was something that had never occurred to either Jon or Anna; and seeing their looks of dismay, Jimsie went on grimly:

"Aye, I see you understand me now. But just to put it plainly, if it should happen that there is anything else she wants from any of us there's not a woman or child in the village could go on those rocks without being in danger from her. And as for the men, there's not one of them would be safe if she threatened to get what she wants by singing him on to his death on The Drongs."

"But what more *could* she want?" Anna asked fearfully; and with a tap of his knife on the carved figure of the mermaid, Jimsie answered:

"Who can say what might come into the head of a creature like this? Maybe she'll not really want anything from us – except the feeling of power it will give her to know that she can blackmail us into doing her will. And *that's* the danger from her now, Anna. That's why you *must not* give her the comb."

"But what about her threat to drown the men?" Anna cried. "What else *can* I do except to yield to that?"

"You can go on with the battle of wills that's been taking place between the two of you," Jimsie said. "And this time, you must make sure that you win that battle.

You must find some way to tame that mermaid so that she can nevermore harm any of us."

"How?" Jon and Anna spoke together, Jon looking doubtfully at Jimsie, Anna with a glimmer of hope in her face. But the hope died as Jimsie shook his head, and answered:

"I can't tell you that. There's only one person here who can tell you how to bind a mermaid to your will, and that person is the Howdy."

"But I'm frightened of the Howdy!" Anna exclaimed. Jon said nothing, but it was clear from his face that – even although he was now well-grown boy of thirteen – he, too, was still afraid of the Howdy.

Jimsie bent again to his carving. "Well," he said, "I've given you the best advice I can; and so now you know that there's only one of two things you can do. You can either give in to the mermaid over the comb and so risk bringing disaster on the whole village; or you can learn how to tame her by getting over your fear of the Howdy. You have your choice. But don't forget, you have only three days now before that choice has to be made."

Chapter Eleven

The Howdy's house stood a little apart from the other houses in the village. Inside, it was dim, with all sorts of peculiar smells coming from bunches of dried herbs hanging from the rafters. It had taken Jon and Anna two days to get up enough courage to seek out the Howdy there, and now they did not at all like either the feeling of the place or the way the Howdy looked at them once they had nerved themselves to tell their story.

"You have always run out of my path before this," she grumbled. "And so why do you think now that I will bother to help you? Answer me that. And be sure you give me the right answer, too, or I will not lift a finger to do so."

The right answer? Jon and Anna looked in dismay at one another. Then they looked at the Howdy, and something in the little woman's bright, darting eyes gave Anna an inspiration.

"Because you've seen something of the future already," she said. "And so you know that we are the only ones who *can* tame the mermaid."

The Howdy looked sourly at her. "You've guessed it,"

she admitted. "All along, ever since your Granda left here for fear of the mermaid, I've had glimpses of what the future held for all of you. And it wasn't long after he'd gone, too, that I saw far enough into the future to know that you and your brother would be the ones to come here some day to ask what you have just asked."

With an effort, then, she heaved her fat little self out of her chair, and came up to Jon. She felt the muscles of his arms, and muttered, "Aye, you're strong." She looked at the knife in his belt – the long sharp knife his Granda Eric had sent him. "But will you have the courage," she asked, "to use that knife the way I'll tell you to use it?"

"If I have to," Jon told her, trying not to shrink from the feel of her fingers prodding his arm.

"And you," said the Howdy, turning to Anna, "if I say what must be done to help your brother, will you have the courage for that?"

"If I must," said Anna.

"Then listen," the Howdy told them, "and you *will* be able to tame that mermaid. But only if you do *exactly* as I tell you to do. D'you understand?" Jon nodded, looking at Anna. Anna nodded, looking at Jon; and with her voice now low and eager, the Howdy began to give them her instructions on how to tame a mermaid.

That was far from being the end of it, however, because it was all very well to have such instructions, but – as Jon and Anna both realised very clearly – the problem was in finding a way to carry these out. That, it seemed, was one thing the Howdy could not tell them. Nor could Jimsie Jamieson when, in desperation at last, they went down to the harbour to seek his advice on that matter.

There was nothing left for them to do in the end, in fact, but to argue the case back and forward with one another until they had lit on a plan that they could at least hope would work. And then, having got that far, to swear they would stand by one another no matter what happened when they put the plan into action.

On the following day, then, when they went out to the rocks to summon the mermaid, Anna took her comb with her. Jon, as usual, had his conch shell, and his knife. The two of them went quickly out to the point where they would meet the mermaid; and there, Anna dressed her hair up on top of her head. Then she stuck the comb into her piled-up hair, and stood waiting while Jon blew his summons.

Neither of them spoke while they waited for her, each of them knowing only too well the fear that was in the other's heart. It was only when they saw her coming at last, in fact, that Jon whispered:

"Are you sure, Anna? Are you quite sure you can persuade her?"

"I told you," Anna reminded him. "I'm a girl and she's at least half a woman, and so I know the way her mind works. *I'll* persuade her!"

The mermaid surfaced. Her glance flew to Anna standing in front of Jon, her red hair gleaming in the sun, the green of the comb stuck in it glowing darkly against the red. With a smile of triumph on her face and her eyes fixed on the comb, the mermaid reached up a hand towards it and cried out eagerly:

"It's mine now! It's mine! Give it to me!"

"Yes, you can have it at last," Anna agreed; and with a great sigh of pretended regret, she took the comb out of her hair. For a long moment she stood looking at it; and then, with another great sigh, she added, "Although I still hate to have to give it to you – especially when you don't even know how to wear it properly."

The mermaid looked sharply at her. "What d'you mean by that?" she demanded. "I've had combs before. You saw the golden comb I was wearing that night my song drew you to me; and what was wrong with the way I wore that?"

"Nothing," Anna admitted. "But that was only a small comb, with its teeth set close enough together to grip your hair the way you always seem to wear it streaming loose down your back. This is a big comb, with its teeth set too far apart to get a proper grip on your hair – unless, of course, you wear it piled up on your head the way mine is now."

The mermaid's wary expression turned to one of doubt. With one hand gripping the rock and the other reaching behind her head, she used her free hand to draw long strands of her sandy-gold hair to the top of her head.

"Like this?" she asked.

Anna stood with her head on one side, considering the effect. "Not quite," she said at last. "It has to come higher yet. Look—" Kneeling down to bring herself nearer to the mermaid, she offered, "I'll show you how. If you sit here beside me on the rock, in fact, I'll do it for you."

The mermaid drew back a little. "Why should you?" she demanded. "I would not try to make any of my sisters look more beautiful by offering to dress *her* hair!"

"You don't have to tell me that," Anna pointed out to her. "You've said more than enough already to let me know how jealous you all are of one another. But *I'm* not jealous of your beauty. And since I must give you my comb, I do at least want to know it will be shown off to its best effect."

The mermaid looked from her to Jon, standing watching the two of them with his hand laid lightly on the knife in its sheath on his belt. "Make him go away, then," she ordered. "I will not come out of the water for such as him to see."

Anna turned her head to look up at Jon. "Do as she says," she told him.

Jon turned from her and the mermaid. Seconds later, he was lost to sight behind a big rock. They heard sounds that seemed to show he was scrambling even further away; and it was then that the mermaid slid upwards to seat herself on the rock beside Anna.

"Now," she said, "you can dress my hair and put the comb properly in it."

Anna moved to kneel behind her. Gently she drew the green comb through the mermaid's long wet hair; and, like a cat being stroked, the mermaid quivered with pleasure in the feeling. Anna laid the comb down. She parted the mass of hair hanging down the mermaid's back. She took one half of this mass in her left hand, the other half in her right hand.

"There," said she "it's all ready now to be gathered up on top of your head." She was glancing back over her shoulder as she spoke, towards the rock where she had last seen Jon. And Jon, as the two of them had planned, had not gone away. She could see him at that moment, peeping out of hiding; and with her hands fiercely tightening their grip on the mermaid's hair, she screamed at the top of her voice:

"Jon!"

Jon bounded towards her, his knife ready in his hand. The mermaid jerked at the sound of her scream and pulled madly against the grip on her hair. The pull took her sliding off the rock, with Anna still holding on like grim death being dragged behind her. Jon reached them before Anna could be dragged into the water. Dropping his knife to the rocks, he flung himself down beside Anna; and, closing his hands over her hands, he added all his strength to the grip that she had on the mermaid's hair.

She screamed against the pain of this added pull against her scalp, and furiously thrashed her great tail in the effort to break loose. But fisher boys and girls like Jon and Anna are hardy beyond the normal, and Jon was very strong for his age. The mermaid could not break free. She let herself sink downwards, and then gave a tremendous jerk that was intended to pull them down with her. But Jon and Anna were ready for this, and as she jerked downwards, they jerked upwards. The mermaid surfaced, and as she did so, Jon shouted:

"It's not your life we want. We won't kill you."

She twisted her head to stare up at him, her face ugly with hate, her eyes like green fire in the paleness of her face. She opened her mouth to speak, but Jon had reached out one hand for his knife; and before she could utter a word, he had laid the whole length of its long, sharp blade against the mass of hair gripped in his other hand.

"I'll cut," he threatened. "The instant you try to break away again, I will cut off all your hair with one stroke of this blade – unless you give us the three wishes it is in your power to give."

The mermaid became suddenly still as death. "Who told you?" she whispered. "Who told you I could grant three wishes? And who told you I have no magic without my hair?"

"It makes no difference who told us," Jon said grimly. "You are tamed now. And I warn you, my knife is very sharp. So which is it to be? Will I cut, and destroy your magic? Or will you give us the three wishes?"

"Your choice is no choice at all," the mermaid said sullenly. "Am I to be the laughing-stock of my sisters with my hair cut off and all my magic gone? Speak up, and tell me your first wish."

Jon looked at Anna. She was holding as hard as ever to the mermaid's hair, but she was smiling now. He smiled back at her, drew a deep breath, and said "I wish that no man, woman, or child, of our village will ever again be drowned at sea."

The mermaid ground her teeth in rage at the way this first wish had struck right at the heart of her power; but the knife was still laid against her hair, and so all she could do was to say sullenly, "Granted. Now make your second wish."

"I wish," said Jon, "that no boat I ever build will be wrecked at sea."

"Granted." Once more the mermaid gave her sullen agreement; and once more, Jon glanced at Anna. He had made the wishes so far, just as they had planned, with one for the whole village and then one for himself. Now the plan called for Anna to make her wish; and eagerly she told the mermaid:

"I wish my Granda Eric would come home again."

The mermaid stared curiously at her. With contempt in her voice, she remarked, "That's a very small wish!"

"It's all I want," Anna told her. "And the moment you grant it, we'll let you go."

Relief shone in the mermaid's face, wiping out the hatred in it and leaving it once again beautiful. "Granted!" she cried. "Oh, granted!" And the moment she spoke, Jon and Anna released their hold on her.

Down, down into the water she sank. Anna picked up the precious green comb she had fought so hard to keep, and proudly put it back into her hair. Jon sheathed his knife, and waited with Anna to see if the mermaid would show herself again; but she was gone for good, it seemed, because not another single sign of her did they see.

"That's it, then," said Jon. "This time, Anna, it really is all over." And so it was – so far as the mermaid was concerned, at least. But even so, as Jon and Anna soon found to their cost, there were other matters yet to be faced as the result of that morning's work.

For a start in these other matters, there was the fact that Jimsie Jamieson had been very worried by all that Jon and Anna had told him. The Howdy, also – to do her justice – had become very agitated by the thought that she had consented to instruct a boy of thirteen and a girl of twelve over an action that might very well cost them their lives. All the time Jon and Anna had been having their battle with the mermaid, then, Jimsie had been worrying to the point where he decided to go and see the Howdy himself.

"I shouldn't have sent these children to you," said he regretfully. "And you should never have told them what you did. It'll be on my conscience and on yours too, Howdy, if that mermaid drowns them." All of which brought the Howdy's agitation to the point where nothing would satisfy her but that the two of them should rush straight away to Jon and Anna's home to see if it was still possible to stop them trying to carry out the Howdy's instructions.

"But it's an hour since the two of them went out this morning!" cried Kristine; and Sarah, too, cried out in alarm. Within seconds of that, the two of them were rushing out to sound this alarm all over the village; with the result that boats were put out from the harbour to search for what everyone feared would be the drowned bodies of Jon and Anna, and on their way home over the rocks they were met by every single soul who could manage to scramble out there to their help.

There was a fearsome amount of explaining to do then, with a great deal of blame for Jon for having summoned the mermaid in the first place, and the same amount of blame for Anna for having made matters worse by refusing to give up her comb. But once everyone had calmed down, of course, there was an equal amount of praise for the way they had defeated the mermaid in the end, and also for the way that Anna had gained time for the herring fleet to have a good season.

At the end of that mermaid summer, also, when the herring fleet came home and the men of the boats heard the story, they made such a fuss of Jon and Anna that, far from being angry with them, Robert Anderson was pleased beyond measure to think it was his son and his daughter who had finally made the village safe from the mermaid.

And made it safe, they certainly had because, from that day forward, there was no single person from that village who was ever drowned at sea. As time went on, also, the work that Jon did in the boatyard became famous because, all along that coast it was noted, no boat that he had a hand in building was ever wrecked. All that, however, still lay far in the future, and it was long before these first two wishes came true, that Anna had *her* wish granted.

It was only three months after the mermaid had been tamed, in fact, that Eric Anderson came home to his family – which made it three years to the day since he had left them. And it was Anna who was the first to see him.

Chapter Twelve

Anna's first thought, once everything was over, was that she must write to her Granda Eric to tell him all about it. But then, it struck her, what would be the point to that when he was certain to come home anyway, and it would be so much more enjoyable to tell him the whole story at first hand? She was impatient, all the same, to discover just when he would come home; and, it seemed to her, it was only the Howdy who could tell her that.

Fortunately, too, she no longer had any fear of the Howdy now that she had realised how harmless the little woman really was. As for the Howdy herself, she was once again full of her own importance, and quite proud therefore to be able to tell Anna that Eric would come home in exactly three months from the date that the mermaid had been tamed.

"Because," said she, "you that's kept such good account of passing time with your letters to him, you must know very well that three months from that date will mean that his absence has lasted for three years. And, as I told your grandmother one day, 3 is the number that rules the fate of Eric Anderson – 3 being the number that is at the root of all magic. And there is no denying, is there, that magic has been at work in everything that has happened since he dared the mermaid to take her revenge on him?"

No, Anna agreed, there was no denying that. And so, with the Howdy's words firmly in her mind, it was not surprising that she was the first to see Eric come swinging down the road to the village, looking just as he had on the day he had left it, with his kitbag on his shoulder and his one gold earring glinting in the low sun of the winter's day. With a shout that brought Sarah running to the door of the house, she sped to meet him; and with cries of welcome on their lips, the rest of the family followed after.

From all over the village then, other people came hurrying. Robert took Eric's kitbag as he shook hands with them all; and it was like this, escorted by a whole mob of Eric's friends, that the family reached home again. As many as possible crowded in with them then to share in the homecoming, with The Oldest Fisherman well to the fore and the Howdy crowding on his heels. The Howdy, you may be sure, was not going to miss anything.

Robert managed to find a seat of some kind for each one. Sarah and Kristine rushed to make tea for them all. There was a great hubbub of talk and laughter, until Jimsie Jamieson finally managed to make himself heard above all this.

"And tell us, Eric," he called, "what was it that

changed your mind about coming back to the village?"

Everyone fell silent then – and not only because they wanted to hear what Eric would have to say to this, but also because there had been time by then to notice that Eric was not the man he had been when he had left the village. He was well, certainly, and his manner was just as bluff and hearty as it had been before. But there was one thing missing from him, and that was his laugh – the big rich laugh that everyone had always so much enjoyed hearing.

There were many looks of curiosity then, as Eric put down his tea and prepared to answer this question, and even more curiosity when he started by calling Anna to him. She came obediently to stand at his side, and watched along with everyone else as he put his hand inside his jacket and drew out a thick bundle of letters.

"D'you recognise these?" he asked her, holding out the bundle for her to see; and – a bit shyly in the face of all that company – Anna told him:

"Of course I do. They're the letters I kept writing to you all the time you were away."

"Aye," said Eric. "And that were waiting for me at the Seamen's Mission, every time my ship got back to its home port." With a great sigh, he put the letters back inside his jacket, and looked from Anna to the rest of the company. "It's a lonely life, the sea," he said; and everyone there could sense then that there was a story coming. They settled back into their chairs, the way people do when they have this feeling. Eric drew Anna down to sit beside him while he waited for them to settle; and then he went on with the story they were all expecting.

"Aye," he said, "even when you have your shipmates all around you, the sea's a lonely life when you're parted from a good wife like Sarah and all the rest of the fine family I have. But there was one thing that used to make me a little less lonely, and that was these letters I got from Anna. I was always very touched too, when I read at the end of every one of them, the plea she had written there: "Please come home soon," it said; and very often I was on the point of yielding to that plea. But once I had left home, of course, the only way I could see to keep myself safe was to make a vow I would never return. And so I made that vow. But then came a night just three months ago when I was on a voyage that gave me a very strange experience – so strange, indeed, that you'll hardly believe it."

Eric paused at this point, and looked at the faces around him as if doubting whether he should continue with his story; and it was Jimsie Jamieson who resolved that doubt for him.

"Go on, Eric," he encouraged, "there's nothing you could say about the sea that would surprise me; and I, for one, will believe you."

Eric nodded his thanks at Jimsie. "Well, then," he went on, "that night was a calm and clear one, with hardly a breath of wind in it. You can hear for miles at sea, as you know, on a night like that; and every man who was awake then, *did* hear something. It was a voice, they said, the sound of a voice singing. They swore to that, in fact; and they swore too, that it was a song without words, sung in the sweetest voice you could ever in your life imagine hearing."

Eric paused again to give yet another searching look around the company, and in the small silence while he did so, Anna thought to herself, *It was the mermaid. It must have been the mermaid!* Beside her, Eric's voice went on:

"But I, too, was awake that night, and I too heard that song. And it was *not* a song without words. I heard very clearly, in fact, the words that voice sang. Over and over again I heard them, and they were the very words that Anna had written in her letters – "Please come home soon, Please come home soon." And I tell you, my friends, there was just no resisting her plea then. Indeed, I could hardly wait for that voyage to end; and the moment it did, I made the fastest time I could back here, to where I am now with you all."

Now Sarah had been listening to all this as intently as everyone else. She had smiled at Eric's mention of her name, but then she had begun to look bewildered by the solemn way he had been speaking. Not once, in fact, had he given even a hint of a smile as he told this tale, and when he finished still without a smile on his face, she demanded:

"Then why don't you look happier about *being* home?"

"How can I," Eric asked in his turn, "when I know very well it must have been the mermaid who sang me home? How could any man be happy coming home to the very danger he hoped to be able to avoid? You know very well too, Sarah, how that danger will catch up with me. And so how can I be happy knowing that the only thing lying ahead of me is another parting from you and all the rest of the family?"

As one person, then, everybody there turned to look at Jon and Anna. And they, of course, were more than ready to tell *their* tale. You could have heard the fall of a feather, too, so quiet did everyone keep as they took it in turns to speak. There was not a movement among all those there, either, except for the sideways glance of eyes at Jimsie Jamieson and the Howdy when the telling came to their part in the story. Eric himself listened like a man in some sort of dream; and at the end of it, he neither moved nor spoke for a long, long moment. When he broke his silence, too, it was not to Jon or to Anna that he spoke, but to the Howdy; and to her he said:

"You spoke in riddles when I came to see you before I left home. And for three years, I've wandered the world looking for presents to send to the family; looking for the kind of things that might be the answer to these riddles. And it seems I haven't done too badly, after all. Have I now, Howdy?"

"Indeed, you have not," said the Howdy, preening herself as she saw the awed glances being cast at her.

"Because I have to tell you, Eric, I couldn't have spoken any plainer to you at the time. But even so, the minute I saw Jon's conch shell, I had the feeling that you were on the right track. The minute I saw the knife and the comb, too, I was sure of that. And so I haven't done so badly either, have I?"

"That's true," said Eric, smiling a bit at the conceit of the little woman.

Slowly then, he got to his feet and stood looking at Jon and Anna. He reached out his right hand to Jon, and shook hands with him, gripping his hand hard, the way he would have gripped the hand of a man. And indeed, it seemed to everyone there, in that moment Jon did become a man. Then he turned to Anna, gathered her into his arms, and gave her the great warm embrace she had been longing for three years to have from him. Solemnly, after that, as if he were performing some sort of ceremony for people who had never before met either of them, he put a hand on Jon's shoulder and told everyone:

"This is my grandson, Jon Anderson, who is braver than any man I have ever met. And this," he went on, with a hand coming up to rest on Anna's shoulder, "this is my granddaughter, Anna Anderson, who is as brave as her brother, and who has also more wit to her than any woman I have ever met."

Jon blushed. Anna blushed. There was a sudden burst of excited talk and laughter; and it was then that Eric also laughed. Loud and rich that laugh boomed out, just the way that everyone had always enjoyed hearing it; just the way, everyone realised, that he would continue to laugh now that he knew all his troubles were over at last.

"Well," said he when he had finally finished laughing, "it looks as if I'll live to a ripe old age after all and die in my bed yet – thanks to these two grandchildren of mine. And oh, what a story they'll have to tell *their* grandchildren!"

Both Jon and Anna laughed again at this, neither of them being in the least able to imagine a day when they would be as old as their grandfather. But everyone does grow old, of course, and so there did come a time when they were both grandparents.

Jon had moved away from the village before then, to a place that had a bigger boatyard than the one where he had served his apprenticeship. But Anna loved the village too much to leave it; and so, when her grandchildren visited her there, she did indeed tell them the story of that mermaid summer. And always, too, when she told it to them, she wore her green jade comb in her hair so that they could see for themselves the colour of the mermaid's eyes – and realise too, the beauty of the comb and understand from this why the mermaid should have been so determined to have it.

Her hair was white by that time, of course, instead of red, but there was still a great shining mass of it and the dark green glow of the comb stood out very well against that pure and shining white. Sometimes too, after she had told the grandchildren that story and then put them to bed, Anna would go to the door of her house, and stand there looking out to where she could see The Drongs sticking dark and jagged out of the water.

Faintly then, she would hear the mermaid's song in the way you hear a sound when you put a shell to your ear. But she was never afraid when this happened; because, now that *her* will had been proved stronger than the mermaid's will, the song was no longer a dangerous one that called her out towards the sea. It was one, instead, that sounded only with the sweet, wild notes of freedom, the freedom of creatures that live apart from humankind, and so apart also from human care and sorrow.

Or so Anna liked to think, at least. It seemed to her, too, that there was something in the song that told her she and the mermaid could now even be friends; and this was an idea that much appealed to her. It so happened, also, that Jon had made her a gift of his conch shell before he left the village, which meant it would have been quite easy for her to summon the mermaid. But even so, she always decided, it would be much better for her to leave the shell in the safe hiding-place she had found for it.

How could she tell, after all, what *would* happen if she did decide to use it again?

But supposing the grandchildren discovered the shell's hiding-place – what then? This was the other question Anna sometimes asked herself when she heard the mermaid's song; and the answer she always found to it was that she would face that trouble when it came – if it ever did come.

By all accounts, then, this must have been the sensible way to look at things, because it was not a problem that Anna ever had to face. Also, since all this happened so long ago, with no one ever again seeing any sign of the mermaid, the chances are that the hiding-place of the conch remained secret not only from Anna's grandchildren, but from everyone else who has ever lived in that house since their time.

On the other hand, when you come to think of it, maybe it was found, and the person who discovered it had the good sense not to do anything with it. Or maybe they did not know how it could be used to summon the mermaid. Either that or they did know, and did not have nerve enough to send out the three-times call. Any of these possibilities, in fact, could be the reason for the mermaid never being seen again. But as to which of them is the right one – well, who could give the answer to that?